JOURNEY of the RED BLOODED

JAMES G. MAHONEY JR.

 iUniverse®

JOURNEY OF THE RED BLOODED

iUniverse books may be ordered through booksellers or by contacting:

iUniverse
1663 Liberty Drive
Bloomington, IN 47403
www.iuniverse.com
1-800-Authors (1-800-288-4677)

ISBN: 978-1-5320-6668-9 (sc)
ISBN: 978-1-5320-6669-6 (e)

Library of Congress Control Number: 2019902416

Print information available on the last page.

iUniverse rev. date: 02/27/2019

D own in a remote far off village lives two brothers, named Caleb a skilled hunter of the village and a younger brother Sceiro who is but the wee age of ten. The two live in a small cottage on the outskirts as is needed for Caleb so that he may be close to the woods for hunting. The two live alone there together as their mother passed away and their father went missing shortly after Sceiro was born. As is common to happen to those who travel in the woods, a great many dangers lie in wait as it it inhabited by ferocious beasts not just deer squirls and rabbits. But wolves, bobcats, and bears among other things. Today though Sceiro is not tilling the vegetable garden. He is getting some special attention by the other village mothers. So as not to be in earshot of the meeting taking place,

As Caleb sits and listens to the arguing and commotion taking place, one village farmer stands out above the rest," We all knew this day would come sooner or later, I really don't see the problem."

Herdsman responds," The problem is who can go to the city of parchments with the boy?"

Baker chimes in," Neither is it a short distance nor is it a safe journey, and we can't send many as it is time of the harvest soon."

Finally a loud sigh is heard," ahh" and the room goes silent. And after a moment the village elder who let out the sigh speaks," As it has been said it is the coming of the harvest so many are needed here. And it has been said it is a long and dangerous way to the city … it seems to me what is needed is someone who is young and strong, but this person must also be experienced and brave."

With that statement caleb finally stands and speaks," its not all that complicated … he's my little brother, it makes sense that I be the one who takes him."

The village treasurer exclaims," we can't let caleb go he is the village's best hunter, meat and furs for the winter are just as important as the harvest.

Tredge a village guardsman states," it makes more sense to send a hunter, guard members can't be spared and a hunter is already aware of the dangers of the path through the woods … besides I wouldn't mind being relieved of Caleb and his vexing protests for fortifying the village boarders. As I've said many times there is nothing wrong with our boarders."

Caleb responds," well we do agree on one thing, a hunter is best suited for the job … not some fat lazy guardsman who thinks our village is completlely safe with just a moat trench and a few manned bridge crossings."

Tredge," why you son of a …" cut off by village elder," then it is decided, Caleb will travel with the boy … his brother, and let that be the end of it."

Meanwhile Cirena is keeping Sceiro busy with some unique errands. After the other mothers had their fun dressing him in some cute cloths whilst giving him some teasing, Sceiro was given permission to collect herbs and flowers. Which is rare especially for a boy to have the opportunity to do. Very near finishing his collection Sceiro happens to spot a shimmering viper. Shimmering vipers have a skin that changes color to camoflage it, so it is rare to find one. Thusly Sceiro is highly anxious, especially when he notices that this particular viper has happened to not be aware of his presence. As Sceiro creeps up behind the viper, he removes his shirt so as to avoid its poisonous bite. Then at just the right moment, Sceiro pins down the viper with his foot and grabs it by the base of its head, shirt in hand. At this moment Cirena calls for Sceiro to come back, he's been foraging for some time and doesn't want him to stray too far. So Sceiro ties the viper up inside his shirt so he can safely carry it back, then chuckles to himself as he makes his way to return with his hard work and rare prize. When Sceiro arrives back the other women begin to scold him, thinking he lost his new shirt while away. As he tries to explain that he did not lose his shirt he simply took it off, they refuse to listen and proceed to hold him down to give him a lashing with a birch branch. Luckily Cirna halts them in protest to hear him out, having just noticed his return. He presents her his foraging bag, which is filled with lilacs, buttercups, hayweed, clover, mysterium, as well as various types of mushrooms and scented holly berry … along with his missing shirt. Cirena, curious to know whats in his shirt starts to untie it, assuming there are more herbs. Its at this moment Sceiro objects, explaining the contents of his tied shirt. Upon learning of his fortunate capture Cirena feigns a grin while the other women gasp in awe and some of them even appologize for their rash decision to discipline him.

In the citystate of the labyrinth law cube maze known as the city of light. In the capital resides the Hall of Records where Trisdin meets to speak with Tikrah, an assasssin for hire. Trisdin is an official for the capital, who is interested in obtaining specific records pertaining to the heir to the cubemaze's prize at the end of the labyrinth. Tikrah on the other hand has more devious designs for the valuables he stands to gain for his endeavors.

Tikrah," so what is this news of a missing codex thats been found?"

Trisdin," there's not much, its all very hush hush."

Tikrah," then why did you disturb me you bothersome trifle."

Trisdin," because you know how to get people to talk, you know people who can get away with doing things … things that get people like me killed or sent to prison."

Tikrah," I don't bother with such miniscule work …"

Trisdin," but for a codex? …"

Tikrah," not for might be, not for simple rumors and whispers."

Trisdin," then point me in the right direction of who can find out more, so people don't know I'm poking around."

Tikrah," I do know someone like that … you."

Trisdin," no wait, I can't!"

Tikrah," you don't get it, I'm interested in valuable things. A codex is valuable, and you're already in a good position to obtain the information I need … if you don't well … you know the type of skill set I employ."

Trisdin," and if I refuse."

Tikrah," then get used to the idea of a coffin with alot of flesh eating things, and you will be alive when they start to eat."

Trisdin," fine, try to employ someone and I end up the employee. I need at least three or four days."

Tikrah," talk to the morning sun inn keeper to get in contact with me. If i don't hear anything i'll return here in five days … after that, not to sure what will happen to you."

Sceiro sits at his small little table enjoying breakfast. Cirena," would you like more bacon?"

Meanwhile …

Raize," a months food and drink, two weeks there two weeks back. Three horses, a packhorse and two mounts. Two quivers, fifty arrows, one recurve bow, and one claymore. You should be all set."

Caleb," the claymore isn't necessary, new leather gear would be nice.

Raize," you may be a hunter, but no claymore traveling abroad doesn't work, you take it even if its just for appearances. The new leather gear great … though I suggest for your little brother, chainmail curaiss and cloth. Especially when you get around populated areas."

Sceiro," done …"

Cirena," go wash up and get dressed."

Sceiro," k … Caleb says we're going on a trip!"

Cirena," I know do you know where?"

Sceiro," no, and I asked if it was cuz we were moving, he said no."

Cirena," why would you think that?"

Sceiro," not many people like me or my brother … he has an attitude people don't like. Mostly cuz of the gruff he hears cuz of my marks … they make people uncomfortable."

Cirena," do you know what is said about your marks?"

Sceiro," no, I just overhear him grumbling in his sleep."

Cirena," thats not a nice thing to do eavesdropping on a sleep speaker."

Caleb enters the house," he eat?"

Cirena and Sceiro," yea."

Sceiro," where are we going?"

Caleb," to a city, we have to travel through the forest down briar tunnel rd. so you have to be a scaredy-cat-not, right."

Sceiro," k, can I bring my flute?"

Caleb," yea as long as I can bring my toke."

Sceiro," mhmm."

Six days after the Hall of records meeting, trisdins home.

Trisdin," wait, you don't have to do anything,"

Irugez(assassin)," kit is tired of waiting … you've been deemed a loose end …"

Trisdin," no! I don't know if you work for Tikrah, but I know its late but I have the information he requested …"

Irugez," elaborate, quietly or i'll silence you permanent."

Trisdan," a small distant village, about a three weeks ride from the Library of Symbols, theres supposedly a child with markings on his body … the suspicion is that the kids body is or part of a codex, and is traveling two days now with an older companion to have the possible codex symbols interpreted."

Irugez," and the name of the village?"

Trisdin," Briarhut village."

Irugez," interesting, anything else important come to mind?"

Trisdin," no, it's not what I was hoping to get either … nothing about the heir … umm … unless the kid …"

Irugez," like i csaid loose end," cuts Trisdin's throat.

Eight days into the woods, completely passed through Briar Tunnel Rd. two days ago … now the road is more dangerous being exposed more to larger animals who can move freely across the road.

Caleb," we need to hold up here, it's past mid-day and need to rest before we cross the river bridge."

Sceiro," can we eat?"

Caleb," yea but we need to change first, yours are lightweight don't worry."

Sceiro," I'm really hungry lets eat first, and then i'll play a lil so you can cheif."

Caleb," deal."

Next morning

Caleb," hey get changed you forgot last night."

Sceiro," hey"

Cenvaw(assassin)," shut up."

Tikrah," so thats a codex written on skin."

Lawrnev an assassin leaps out from the woods and throws a dagger. Caleb dodges and rolls to his bow and one of the quivers, quickdraw fires two arrows at Cenvaw. One in the wrist clutching his brother, one in Cenvaw's neck. Lawrnev throws multiple daggers at a time.

Caleb," get a short blade kiddo"

Sceiro," can't argh."

Tikrah," keep him busy, I've placed wolverine scent bombs to aid your escape."

Caleb," you'll both be dead before enough arrive …"

Caleb fires two arrows one sring hesitating Tikrah, and two consecutive barages blocking Lawrnev's dagger throws. Tikrah throws a gord vase bpttle of wolverine odor at caleb, with one wolverine just arriving … Tikrah steals Sceiro's clidesdale, noticing the specific breed is rare as well as more or less the best. Lawrnev afraid of the beast tosses daggers at both it and Caleb, who double fires arrows. He hits an arial dagger and clips lawrnev's left shoulder. Tikrah already off to who knows where with his prize, Lawrnev throws magnesium flare grenades to blind Caleb and the now two wolverines of his escape. Dimness of regular light returns with caleb alone against the wolverines. With two wolverines he takes no chances, three simultaneously a set of at each one. One three round shot, another, another, no more left. Dodgeing and rolling he lost seven arrows from his quiver, he dashes to his horse. A sheildblade and a ¾ long sword, turning to his opponents hoping at least one had fled after the pain of arrows barage, to no avail from the left it stops short. To the right a plunge with the ¾ blade under its chin threw its head … no time let go of the blade, sheild with his left, a right punch to its head. Rolls away picks up a thrown dagger. The remaining beast lunges again, bites down on the sheild blade, caleb viciously stabs and cuts its throat.

Caleb," mother fuck you, who the fuck were they, and where the hell did you pricks go with my lil bro … I'll get cleaned up at the river, keep going get some answers in the city. This one will probably buy a tale," looking at Cenvaw.

Tikrah," it was you and Cenvaw I commissioned who was the other assassin there."

Nexaug," how should I know I was protecting the rivers raft crossing."

Sceiro," are you gonna kill me"

Nexaug," should we are you a bad kid, lol."

Tikrah," shut up Nexaug, I might if I find you useless."

Sceiro," then you won't, I can farm, collect herbs and play music."

Tikrah," mhm."

Nexaug," thats how assassins live, you could be one if you're strong enough."

Tikrah," child who was the other two with you?"

Sceiro," not two just one."

Tikrah," the blade thrower or the bowman?"

Sceiro," the bowman … where you taking me?"

Nexaug," to the assassins citadel of records, your codex marks are very intriguing … a comparison needs to be made."

Sceiro," I was headed to have them interpreted already."

Tikrah," you weren't going to my people though."

Sceiro," whats the difference?"

Nexaug," appropriate use of the facts … the truth."

Sceiro," like killing people."

Nexaug," no …"

Tikrah," shut it brat. You know little of what you speak."

Sceiro," how long til we get there."

Nexaug," three moons."

Sceiro," then unbind me, theres no way I can get away, let me play my flute."

Nexaug," so you play flute."

Tikrah," flute music, no you stay bound that music is a nuisance."

Sceiro," you're a nuisance."

Fifteen days after Sceiro's kidnapping, Caleb finds himself in a holding cell of the southwestern citadel of the city of light city-state.

Sartoc," your story checks out stinky assassin slayer."

Caleb," does that mean someone can help me get my lil bro back or at least the info I need to do it myself."

Sartoc," no we can help … but before that because of why you two were coming, can you identify/write the markings on your bros body?"

Caleb," yea not a single mark on his body escapes my concern, but putting arrows through his captors seems more important if you ask me."

Sartoc," its not … and i have orders to keep you detained if you refuse to accompany me to the Hall of Symbols Library."

Caleb," how long,"

Sartoc," a day and a half to there."

Caleb," fine."

After a long day of rope weaving Ichary gets to relax a little while she smoke burns the fat off of the hydes she has to work into cloths and armor. And thusly so, in her relax time she puffs on her pipe a while and enjoys some floral tea. Ichary is an armor and weapons repair smithery. Because she's apt at her profession she has to travel to do her work, at least until she has enough money to own her own smithery. Whether that be the city or between villages and camps' tents she has yet to decide.

Oxgruf," you bitch the shield set you made me doesn't work, I want my money back."

Ichary," yeah sure thing, and while i'm at it I'll repair/remake your shields just say yea and I'll not snap to."

Oxgruf," wai … t … wha …"

Ichary," sorry is that a no or a yes?"

Oxgruf," um, yes."

Ichary," then be off i'm done with your patronage."

Oxgruf," no, you …?"

Ichary," listen I make good things, I'll not be blamed by how you misuse them understand."

Oxgruf swings his woods battle ax into a table.

Ichary," fine let me see one."

Oxgruf shows her a leather made one. Its loose and easy to tear in its present condition.

Ichary," been swimming with it have we been?"

Oxgruf," no, up in the mountains I were. No water there, so its your blame."

Ichary," mountains, and he says no water does he … my fault is it … well then I guess snow doesn't count as water with you brutes … tis no fault of mine when you play in frozen water dust. But I can retaught the leather for a small stipend if you like?"

Oxgruf," snow … well … but … how much?"

Ichary," ten geo stones."

Oxgruf," thats mad, just favor me, eh dear."

Ichary," nothin doin, five for the job, two more cause its me pipe and tea time, and three for the mark on the table you oaf."

Oxgruf," not a chance."

He moves to strike her with the blunt end of his ax, she cracks a short range leather whip with a debilitating halucinagenic blade tip. Oxgruf falls in a stupper, passes out after a few minutes.

Ichary," well now seems its time to move shop, but first what have we in our pockets, eh."

Oxgruf," ugh, not your … pockets."

Ichary," no, but whats in them be mine they do, so shut it."

As she rumaged threw his pockets and bags, she finds seven geo stones, tobacco a decent amount of smoke, and what looks like a childs puzzle toy object but was made of a unique black metal. No time to ponder she must pack up her own wares and go before she and what has transpired is discovered.

Symbol records official," so these symbols are all the symbols your brother has on his body?"

Caleb," yeah, all i can remember."

Symbol records official," it will take some time, maybe a week to decipher this."

Caleb," i can't wait that long my brother needs help, where would they go with him?"

Sartoc," not sure, its not like assassins to have need to have a bounty on a child."

Caleb," maybe its his marks, they heard I was bringing him here."

Symbol records official," that would make sense. If you want information on assassins you should find a tribesman. Children are sold to assassins for money and a better life for the children."

Caleb," shit, wind chimes village, they're the only village that knew about Sceiro."

Sartoc," well you can't usurp authority there but I can ... lets make a deal, you act as a citadel scrawl which is like me without a badge, and you can shake down any rogues you like, its easy they give in easy and don't like assassins so info gets spit like candy.

Caleb," sounds like a plan, I'm guessing rogues are thieves."

Sartoc," yea."

12 days left to get to the assassins citadel

Nexaug," lets make camp."

Tikrah," still daylight."

Nexaug," the boy is useless if exhausted."

Sceiro," I'm not so weak."

Tikrah," shut it, and his only use is to have his body examined. A dead body with marks I doubt is any different than a live one."

Nexaug," any more comments like that and you'll find yourself not very lively Tikrah."

Tikrah," fine camp it is."

Sceiro," so how bout my bindings, I could go for some smoke, like where am I gonna go?"

Tikrah," no."

Nexaug," i disagree (cuts bonds) play your flute. No smoke too young."

Sceiro," k," starts playing and both Tikrah and Nexaug smell the smoke.

Tikrah," he said no."

Nexaug," how."

Sceiro," my flute is played while I smoke ... care to try."

Nexaug," no."

Tikrah," what are you puffing?"

Sceiro," ground floral mix."

Tikrah," hmm."

Nexaug," is it healthy."

Sceiro," for breath, and it allows me visions when in need. Other than that it calms my heart."

Tikrah," no different than my cactus juice."

Nexaug," or eating my mushroom caps. Anyway play something nice child."

Hartic(rogue)," so how much do you have to pay? I heard you're interested in anything assassin, especially related to a dead one in the same breath as an arrow wounded one?"

Caleb," my pay is not dragging you to a trough and drowning you."

Hartic," ahh fine, alright theres a guy at Lunar Star Inn with a left arm sling and wrappings."

Caleb tosses an assassins throwing dagger," if you're lying I'll find you."

Hartic," I'm not, but with payment you get extra ... his specialty isn't merely throwing these, they're poison tipped."

Caleb," not a problem for me, thanks for the tip."

The symbol records official brings the last codex up from the basement files that are similar to the symbols caleb pointed out.

Zaqua(elder priest)," if these turn out to be the right symbols, then the child might be the reason the labyrinth maze cube exists. It says here, to use the symbols on a six by nine point system to solve the puzzle to reveal and obtain the prize, an object of massive power. But it doesn't say what it is or what it does. I must see the real markings to be sure these are the right matching codexs. And more importantly, need someone to challenge the maze cube to find out what this six to nine point system is."

Symbol records official," that caleb is a bit to brash to do the job right, it would take an assassin or a thief."

One day after leaving Oxgruf's camp. Ichary steering her bull drawn wagon puts down her pipe and begins to fidgit with the puzzlebox a bit.

Ichary," these things are impossible to solve when they're designed the way this one is. The damn symbols none of them match, whatever I'll just head home."

Sartoc stops at a camp on his way to wind chimes village," whats all the commotion."

Dextra," seems Oxgruf got rolled yesterday."

Sartoc," what happened?"

Oxgruf," a damn vixen weapon smith sticky fingered witch stole a symbol tech artifact I planned on bountying with you in fact."

Sartoc," hrmp, the plot thickens. Any ideas what it was, looked like … where she went?"

Oxgruf," nah, she put me down quick … sleep lash it was, dunno, but it was like a cube puzzle … really complex, strange symbols, no directions."

Dextra," she left headed toward your citadel sartoc, surprised you didn't cross her path."

Oxgruf," no, she takes back road paths, she likes anonaminity."

Sartoc," damn two relics two directions, one me. Ox you and your crew wanna hire from me?"

Oxgruf," kinda, but first that box and that girl come first."

Sartoc," I'm saying includes that …"

Oxgruf," listening."

Sartoc," you me and three more of yours continue my way tracking some assassins and a codex, Dextra and the rest get the relic box and the girl and take it to symbols library and help a man named caleb with the directives of the officials."

Oxgruf," Dex?"

Dextra," sounds like a cake walk on my end, sure."

Sartoc," great … and Dextra make sure caleb gets a reassurance his brother will be fine."

At lunar star inn, as caleb watchs for a wounded man, he can't help but think how all this could've been avoided had he just disagreed with bringing his brother here … the two would have continued a peaceful life. Lawrnev enters the dining room sits down with a coffee. Being he's in the citadel, he isn't dressed as an assassin. Though someone else is and makes their way to him, as caleb listens.

Irugez," how'd you get clipped thats not like you."

Lawrnev," he was good real good and the kid is relic marked."

Irugez," and where is the kid?"

Lawrnev," Tikrah made off with him, probably headed back to the citadel to review the symbols."

Irugez," then why are you here, why aren't you tracking them."

Lawrnev," becaus …"

Caleb pins a dagger to the table," cuz he caught an arrow from my bow … where's my brother being taken you say shitheels?"

Irugez," calm down."

Lawrnev," no fuck this asshole he fires toxic broadheads, its why I'm here been sick for days."

Irugez," why they dont kill."

Caleb," one they do if its strong enough, secondly best way to fuckin hunt, anything. And one more thing I have citadel guards … we will talk or you will die."

Lawrnev," fuck you I am dieing."

Irugez," we can talk if you promise to be considerate of my position."

Caleb," what position?"

Irugez," there's a little division in the assassins society. Our job is to maintain order in the world … but assassin legacy bloodlines are factioning and pushing for a powerful royalty system and abolition of original laws and standards."

Lawrnev," and most of the society is in support, only a few of us exist that wanna uphold the old ways and if necessary start a new hidden citadel or find and unused one."

Caleb," so whats my brother have to do with all that?"

Irugez," rumor is he's marked as a codex. The relics are massive objects of power and knowledge, but only those who are blood tied to them."

Caleb," so my brother …"

Irugez," may be … or a link to who is, or a link to a relic."

Lawrnev," and assassins might not be blood tied to the relics but controlling their movement is highly profitable, so is the collecting and influencing those who are."

Caleb," which is why they took my brother."

Krosla, Dextras female lieutenant enters the Inn," Caleb you're needed at the library … the order wants you to select a team to brave the labyrinth. The symbol codex on your brother is related to retrieving a relic at ir's supposed heart."

Caleb," then these two come with us … and go get a thief named Hartic."

Irugez," i'd be better suited to helping to find your brother."

Lawrnev," and i'm not suited for anything I'm not moving."

Caleb," you're both going … I'll give you a remedy … it'll take timeto take effect but you'll recover faster."

Sartoc," do you really think she would head to the citadel of light?"

Oxgruf," no, she probably expressed her leaving to hide her true direction. She sticks to camps and small villages.

Sartoc," well we're headed to Wind Chimes Village."

Oxgruf," thats not her direction too close … prolly Tree Folk Cove."

Sartoc," you know where that is?"

Oxgruf,: yea why what you thinking?"

Sartoc," leave two men with me, take one with you. The two of you should have no problem detaining one girl right."

Oxgruf," thats not a bad idea. Steel-run you're with me, the rest of you stay with him. We come across bulls tracks we've crossed her path."

Tikrah, Nexaug, and Sceiro reach the outside boarder of the assassin's citadel. Unlike the cube labyrinth which is underground and the entrance is encircled by citadels. The assassin's citadels are below it, the maze is the diamond labyrinth because the maze is shaped like a giant diamond. So its a massive highrise citadel on its outer boarders and downsizes its architecture ever inward to the center which is like a small village size of space under where the tip point of the diamond maze construct is.

Tikrah," here we will find out what you're for boy."

Sceiro," huh."

Nexaug," people like you are special."

After passing through the citadel's outer walls, they move through the inner walls, which turns out there are no inner walls. The citadel's outer buildings are the inner walls and they are equiped with all manner of war invasion weapons and supplies, from highest level to lowest level. The next level of buildings which are connected to the first set, are the living quarters. After that theres some space between, before the next set of buildings, which are library and important documents and historical records. As well as a private symbol interpretation library and scroll codexs. But Sceiro wasn't examined there … he was brought to where the diamond tip was. There an elder assassin who lacked the ability to speak was who Sceiro was to meet with. There the markings he has were studied and compared to the codexs and the two relics they have. As the elder makes marks on his writing scroll, all wait intently as the assistants interpret. Sceiro's limbs were copied first, then back, chest, and neck. After the symbols were copied, Sceiro was requested to hold and attempt to solve the relic puzzles, the two they had. One was a cylindrical shaped puzzle, the other was a disk. Its obvious to him that the puzzles are symbol and shape based ... the problem was he had no idea if he was doing something right or not. Shape he understood but symbols were different, he wasn'r raised on what the relic symbols meant, only that they were old. He made the cylinder a cylinder with different symbol placement a number of times then gave up. The disk turned out to be very easy, the disk is a relic thats a codex ... each relic has to be deciphered by a disk. Upon this discovery being that it was lateand no one else noticed it, Sceiro placed the disk and cylinder in his bag ... then asked Nexaug where he could sleep explaining his failure.

The record officials discovered that Sceiro's markings are directions and symbol tech plot points for navigating and solving puzzles and opening construct doors. With this knowledge Caleb with his selected team Irugez, Hartic, and Krosla entered the maze cube to retrieve whatever relics that could be discovered. Meanwhile, Dextra had Lawrnev detained, Caleb ordered he be interrogated about everything assassin. Unbenonced to Irugez as it was under the guise of bedrest for the toxic broadhead.

Lawrnev," here to babysit ... nah I overheard dear old Caleb's request ... just wonder why you didn't explain what you know."

Dextra," more or less the same as you ... see I can tell you're here to watch that Irugez who believes the two relics you have should be sent to where they belong … where as you think they should be ransomed or worse. Well its the same here, as a wind chimes native if you thought I'd let that relic cube puzzlego to that kid you're dead wrong."

Lawrnev," relic cube? … thats not right if thats the case then the cube labyrinth houses something else."

Dextra," yea, the way the mazes are solved determines what relic is obtained, Calebs team will acquire the relic sphere."

Lawrnev," how can you be sure?"

Dextra," been at this a while … we control the symbols library here … and our living codex has the relic cube and when solved she should be free to wield the relic sphere without worry of harm."

Lawrnev," you need a relic codex to translate the relic puzzles and the relic sphere is a puzzle."

Dextra," unless you know the meaning of the living codexs, like we do and puzzles … all puzzles can easily be solved with enough time and patience."

Meanwhile Calebs team makes their way through the maze.

Hartic," we should split into two teams, cover more ground that way."

Irugez," said the thief, the maze alters itself as you solve it, splitting up would make things more difficult."

Krosla," well being that there's more than one relic in this maze, splitting up is what we are doing, Caleb who's best with who?"

Caleb," Hartic and Irugez seem like a good match, you come with me Krosla."

Hartic," the four of us should each have a copy of the symbol codexs in case something happens."

Caleb," remember this isn't a race if you need to back track, do so."

And so they chose their paths and make their way. The cube maze is underground and rests on one of it's corners. Inside, its unlike traditional mazes … its a labyrinth with puzzle doors to solve along the way. After some time making their way through the maze, solving puzzles working their way past traps. Caleb and Krosla come to a massive door.

Krosla," the symbols on this door don't match any of the codexs, but to pass up a find like this … we may never find this door again."

Caleb," these symbols I've seen before, they're music symbols, my brother studies them."

Krosla," do you know them?"

Caleb," i have a basic understanding that's all … these are low these are high, thats the best I got. But maybe it just needs to hear the song, we could belt the tones somehow, well you can I don't sing."

After a few hours of study and trial and error, Krosla harmonies the song right. And they both hear a loud booming, the door unlocked but didn't open. Then a bare stone music sheet exposes itself with a message,'tones so beautiful needs a partner.'"

Krosla," they want an accompanyment."

Caleb," it may not be my brother's flute, but my wooden piccolo should do the trick."

Caleb plays and after he gets it right the door opens to a moderately sized room.

Finally at Wind Chimes Village Sartoc discusses things with the villagers and their elders.

Sartoc," what was the stranger's interest in Sceiro the boy who is relic marked?"

Villagers," no different than ever ... marked or specific unique children are bought or stolen. It's the way of things in this world ... who are we to question it?"

Sartoc," so you know nothing specific?"

Villagers," no."

Sartoc," ever come across any relics?"

Village elder," I have a relic blade in my possesion ... its name is bloodletter, its a four blade tuning fork ¾ short blade."

Sartoc," I have a feeling that we are going to need that, do you mind if I take it off your hands?"

Village elder," by all means if it helps."

Sartoc," you head back to the citadel ... I'm going on to get the kid back from the assassins.

Lieing about going to sleep, as the others slumber ... Sceiro works on using the relic disk to solve the relic cylinder puzzle. Finally, just before sunrise, he finishes the puzzle to its initial solved position which activates the relic. As such the cylinder appears to melt into a liquid and then attachs to Sceiro's wrists like shackle bonds. The bonds are very hot causing Sceiro to cry out in pain," aghh!"

Nexaug," what the hell."

Tikrah," you little prick, we didn't watch what you did to know how it works great fucking job."

As the bonds cool the markings on Sceiro's body are absorbed into the shackles making them the bonds symbols ... and new markings form onto his body.

Qualis(bishop)," keep him from the diamond labyrinth as far as possible ... he's nowhere near ready for this."

Nexaug," so the cylinder was a slave relic?"

Qualis," no ... living codexs are actually bloodline relics, the first relic puzzle they fool around with ... usually by solving it in some fashion binds them to the power of the infinence."

Sceiro," what do you mean infinence?"

Qualis," at this point its not up to you."

Sceiro looks at the relic disk, thinks maybe it can help him remove the bracers. Touchs it, it becomes multiple shards that drive into his neck like a collar, as Sceiro is overwhelmed by visions and knowledge rushing through his mind ... stars and planets colliding, exploding blackholes ripping apart on their own immense uncontrolled gravity.

Sceiro," whahhh!"

Ichary bypassed tree cove village and made camp at the mine entrance by the waterfall. After a drink, she folls a smoke for a change and goes back to fidgiting with the puzzle cube. It begins to glowin a strange way with black light ... she sees a triangle on the sides, presses them for some reasonshe doesn't understand. The relic shines blinding darkness everywhere as it pulls her inside the cube puzzle which has altered into a larger open cube puzzle box with a red liquid sphere at its center, which may very well be Ichary.

Irugez and Hartic travelled far into the maze together. But when they reached a relic door irugez stayed behind because it required swimming and as an assassin he's very cautious. Also Hartic tripped a trap that piked Irugez deep into his shoulder. So Hartic inside the relic room has to choose right to get the real relic. There are three to choose, just before he chooses, another door opens … Caleb and Krosla enter …

Hartic," so two directions one relic room, I wonder just one relic?"

Krosla," I see the relic sphere."

Caleb," according to the translation they are all relics. One per opened door can be taken."

Hartic," sphere, two open pyramids, and a disk. Which do we leave? …"

All of a sudden (around the same time Sceiro was collared and Ichary was trapped by the puzzle cube). A strange gray skinned being with green tribal markings appears …

Hartic," too dangerous take all three," grabs the pyramids," two for one."

Krosla," he's right grab the sphere and disk."

Both leave the direction they came, distrusting Hartic Caleb follows him. As all four of them hear the being's words, "citadels shall be entombed, the labyrinth shall rise, and I Riscao will reign. Here comes a darkness rule over the land none can stop."

Hartic emerges from the water.

Irugez," whats going on

Caleb swims out," stop Hartic now."

Without hesitation Hartic sticks Irugez in the kidney with a hand blade.

Irugez," are you fucking kidding me, hole in my arm now one in my side," pulls two daggers as Hartic continues to escape, throws the daggers ... one hits Hartic in the back the other behind his knee.

Caleb," you okay, we need to keep moving ... gotta catch him, gotta get out of here."

Irugez," I mawred him, he'll be hobbling ... leave me and get him, I'll be fine on my own."

Caleb continues on, and Irugez enters the relic room, Lawrnev quietly follows having slipped Dextra's watch.

Riscao," ah one has come, do you wish to die?"

Irugez," I want to help you, in return that you save my life and heal my wounds, the thief who stabbed me uses drug and poison tipped blades ... I won't survive."

Riscao," lol, you will bring me the relic that contains my new vessel."

Irugez is attcked with strange liquid and transforms into a pale red eyed version of himself.

Oxgruf arrives near Tree Cove Village and crosses Ichary's wagon tracks.

Steel-run," her tracks are here, not leading into the village though, but off towards the river."

Oxgruf," that makes sense she likes privacy when she works ... lets go."

They come to her wagon, but no one to be found anywhere ... all of a sudden a beast, much like resembling a werewolf lunges out. Oxgruf staves off a bite with his ax's long handle ... Oxgruf," kill this ugly fuck Steel-run," who fires three arrows into the beast sending it away.

Oxgruf," fuck is that about, whats going on."

Steel-run notices the open relic cube," this might be why," touchs it and is transformed into a white haired werewolf.

He attacks Oxgruf," not today fuckin prick."

He tosses two hatchets, then swings two one-handed axes maiming what was once Steel-run ... then he beheads it. Then he takes a hyde from the wagon and wraps the cube, paying close attention not to touch it ... ties the hyde like a bag, then notices Steel-run's werewolf body is convulsing toward the head which starts howling as Oxgruf watchs in disillusionment he hears return howls and brush move in the woods ... Oxgruf," time to leave it before I'm forced to eat it," and takes his horse and flees.

All the people in the city-states surrounding the buried maze cube that is now rising to the surface, surround the rising structure in awe. Dextra met with Krosla who handed him the relic sphere and explained the unfolding events, which were contrary to the way the wind chimes villagers believed and worked toward.

Dextra," Its fine, word has it that tree cove village is overrun with dog beasts so our living codex solved the cube and needs to be freed with the relic sphere, which will also make her a living god."

Krosla," Hartic has two others, two open pyramids and a relic disk."

Dextra," where is he and Caleb?"

Krosla," don't rely on the thief to show up willingly …
Caleb is on his tail."

Dextra," so we should get back to the village then I bet
that oaf Oxgruf will come through for us."

Krosla," yea, this place is getting some renovations, bad
idea to stick around."

Caleb fires a warning shot with his bow at Hartic's coat
sleeve. He halts doesn't turn around.

Caleb," where do you think you're going with those."

Hartic," the assassins pay a high price for these."

Caleb," well they didn't pay for my lil brother, so I take
those as bargaining payment … if they want those they'll
trade me my brother."

Hartic," how bout I let you come along with me to the
citadel … I have business there, you have business there …
we can watch eachother's backs."

Caleb," fine … I'll hold onto one of those to ensure we
stick together."

Hartic," hrm, no trust in the world, such a sad thing but
okay. I can't really make much protest with such accurate
arrows at my back."

Caleb," well we need to hurry this place is going to
hell."

As the four leave the city-state in two separate
directions, the rest of the public on their knees in prayer as
all the citadels sink into the ground while other new dark
citadels rise up from the ground like the maze cube had.

Riscao," all of you who are in awe and prayer," dark
energy and smoke fills the crowd, all turn into cloaked

ghouls. And now vampire Lawrnev goes to seek out the active relic cube.

Back in Briar Hut Village, Tredge is reviewing accounting reports when a messenger bursts in.

Messenger," reports of impending war between the city states ... talk of it may be necessary for outside villages to choose sides."

Tredge," we will choose the side that is right and just."

Messenger," thats not up to you, the elders have called for a meeting."

Tredge," we'll see how things in this camp are run after the facts and logic are discussed."

Elsewhere in the village Cirena discusses the realities of the new dangers that exist.

Cirena," with so much violence how will poor Sceiro stay so tender. Not to mention ... how will our little village hold off the tide of the change of being ruled."

Cirena thinks,' maybe I should take the relic tome to the altar shrine where it'll be safe. If it falls into the wrong hands things will only get worse.'

Village woman," Tredge will make sure things are ok, we never should have let Caleb and Sceiro journey ... that's prolly the cause."

Cirena, knowing she's partially right doesn't respond.

An elder, knowing Cirena's thoughts asks her to wait til after the meeting ... she's expected to attend.

Tredge," the question at hand is who is the justified side of this impending war?"

Raize," honestly, no one knows, the word is that there's strange occurances and it seems to be alot about relics."

Tredge," relics this relics that, just old wives tales."

Elder," Tredge is right, his assessment of the war's direction and our stance in it is best left in his hands ... that being said. Raize and Cirena can make sure the tome is placed in a protected hidden location, until needed if needed."

Tredge," I suppose that makes sense, if if it can be used as a diplomatic foothold it's best kept safe."

Raize," that all being said ... while I'm away, behind the river trenchs and bridge crossings?"

Tredge," this again our defences are fine, Caleb is insane, too much heart changing in his blood."

Raize," you might be right, but I agree with him, so have a short wall put in place with archer post positioned ... it should at least be halfway complete by the time Cirena and I return."

Tredge," this is bullshit."

Raize," I could give a damn, when it comes to the guardsmen I run things and expect no dissent when I give good improvement orders ... get it done or someone else will."

Tredge," ..."

Elder," (chuckles)"

Heavy breathing ... "ahh"

Sceiro," whos there?"

"What"

Sceiro," over here."

Sceiro meets an ocean blue Ichary who seems to have trouble breathing as if her body has no oxygen in her at all, she's just blue blood infinite non stop. Sceiro is orange complexioned as if he's hot sulfur skinned. Ichary swings at him ... right through his body like a ghost.

Ichary," great help you'll be, are you real or am I cracking?"

Sceiro," I've been attacked by relics."

Ichary," oh ... well join the club, I'm ones prisoner, I have what I need from it, now I just have to get out of here ... do you know anything ... huh."

Sceiro is gone.

Oxgruf nearly to wind chimes village, sees Dextra and Krosla enter the camp. Before he starts the rest of the way, a werewolf who tracked him lunges out ... its a tussel on the ground and Irugez divides the two and together they slay the werewolf ... but for Oxgruf not unscathed. Which is why he makes no inquiry to Irugez or his condition, also cause he dressed as a guard.

Oxgruf," tusselled onto my own ax, look at that, grh."

Irugez," you'll live, that Dextra has a relic

Oxgruf," let's go find out who'll pay the best other than assassins."

Irugez," agreed."

Caleb and Hartic are halfway to the assassins citadel stop to share a smoke of herb by the fire.

Hartic," making it out of the city was rough ... who'd've thought ghouls would really exist."

Caleb," not just any ghouls they were the citadel's people."

Hartic," yeah, that bow of yours came in handy."

Caleb," yea, your not bad with those two short blades ... I mean for a thief, lol."

Hartic," lets get some rest."

Caleb," wait … those relics, lets have a look, try and solve'em."

Hartic," be my guest waste our money."

Caleb studies the disk and pyramids that are open," its mathematical, a mathing symbol game."

Sometime goes by, and Caleb figures out how to close the pyramids. Upon closing the second one the pyramids lock into Caleb's hands through his flesh, points jutting out of the center of his palms, bases jutting out the backs of his hands. Also he undergoes electric shocks, falls unconcious. Hartic who watched everything also saw that the disk ripped apart and left in its place is an all seeing eye relic. Hartic places it inside his coat.

Hartic," must be better priced."

Raize and Cirena on their way to the altar shrine were ambushed by ghouls. Raize fought hard to keep them held back, Cirena opened the relic tome and spell summoned holy fire destroying them. After their interlude with those decrepit interlopers, Cirena thinks maybe holding onto the book is best.

Cirena," should we?"

Raize," yes upon the altar only you or I may remove it."

Cirena," and the fable … once placed upon the altar the children of the elders will be powerful and yet slaves."

Raize," nonsense … our tribe is slave to no one."

After leaving wind chimes village, Sartoc has had to fight various battles that has him perplexed. First a wave of werewolf beasts, which was more than enough alone to get him to wield the blade known as bloodletter. After that he encountered a few packs of ghouls which aren't easy to kill, unlike primal werewolves, ghouls are moderately intelligent. But the most worrysome part is that bloodletter appears to not allow shed blood to fall, instead it looks locked inside the four blades like a continuously condensing rod.

Dextra," now we need to solve the puzzle of the relic to use it."

Krosla," yes but the story of the relic sphere is that its already solved."

Dextra," well …"

Oxgruf," hey any food at this party?"

Krosla," what is it oaf kinda busy."

Oxgruf," know anyone pricing out for an open cube relic with a sphere law center and transmoging people into wolf beasts?"

Dextra," yea, show me."

Oxgruf taking out the open relic cube. Krosla takes out the sphere … right away the sphere attracts to the cube relic and fits the blood sphere, combining. Which releases Ichary who returns with four sphere cresents on her wrists and the cube becomes a dymo (3-D asterix) right away Irugez grabs the dymo.

Irugez," I'll be taking my leave."

Oxgruf," woah now hold on thats technically my relic property since it started as the cube."

Dextra," I agree," lunges a dagger in Irugez's direction.

Irugez uses his hand, opens Dextra's neck and drinks. At this time Oxgruf notices the full moon, and he begins to change. Krosla and Ichary understanding things are getting bad have had enough. Ichary armed with relic weapons forces gravity wells to pull the clouds down into rain, and both werewolf Oxgruf and Irugez must retreat to flee the forming quicksand."

Caleb awakens to a breakfast eating Hartic.

Hartic," morning sleepy."

Caleb looks at his hands the relics are still there. As he brings his hands together, an electricity orb begins to form. Quickly he parts his hands.

Caleb," what the fuck."

Hartic," now I see why they're so desired."

Caleb," where's the disk?"

Hartic," gone … destroyed."

Caleb," no bargaining chips then."

Hartic," we've got your hands, how attached to them are you, lol."

Caleb," hehe … any plans on the best way to get seen without losing my hands?"

Hartic," well its obvious they're active relics … if things go bad, clap … lol."

Vailez," aren't we supposed to be building a wall?"

Tredge," I had archer posts set up thats half of it."

Vailez," technically, yea i suppose it is … but?"

Tredge," we're fine we always …"

Villagers," ahh."

Tredge and vailez rush outside to the towns perimeter. To see two hundred ghouls invading. Vailez wastes no time and alerts the camp and the guards to defend the village.

After a grueling battle, with six of the guardsmen turned and killed the men go to bury the bodies.

Tredge," no burn them, they're disease spreading and burning is faster ... Vailez is right after they're burned get to work on a short wall and scouts search the outside area for invaders ... report back to Vailez.

Zaqwa and Xertic speak about their decisions and parts they played in all of this. As city of light record officials they shoulder alot of responsibility for the latest of events befalling the people.

Xertic," what I've caused is not repairable ... I've brought forth a dark god simply because I thought I understood the relics and their purposes."

Zaqwa," its not your fault its mine for not watching more closely, for not helping better to interpret the symbols."

Riscao is reveling in the constant violence taking place as the third of the citadel's people who didn't turn, fight off the ghouls with no hope of ending in sight.

Riscao," to any who wish to join my flock with status, I require special skills or knowledge of rare things and relics."

Meanwhile back at the assassin's citadel Nexaug is trying to make sense and understand the events that took place in enslaving Sceiro.

Qualis," its good the boy is resting, these trying times and his position are immense."

Nexaug," those bracers were designed to turn the disk into a collar ... its brutal."

Tikrah enters the inner sanctum," there's a report of a strange blade wielder headed this way, which was a rew days ago ... and today not far away strange lightening has been seen with two people who were spotted in the area headed this way it appeared."

Qualis," an invasion."

Nexaug," the boy had a companion ... but neither report sounds like him from Tikrah's earlier description of him."

Tikrah," its possible its him now that you remind me ... he looked highly determined and is very skilled especially in a fight."

Qualis," order the brigades to take open defensive positions."

Ichary," I have the relic sphere and full control of it. Now is the time to collect people's bodies to increase my power ... doing so will leave them as banshee ghosts."

Krosla," you've already absorbed the whole of wind chimes village. And with my relic charm necklace I control those spirits."

Ichary," Oxgruf that oaf is a werewolf now ..."

Krosla," yea so?"

Ichary," I wonder how strong I'd be if I absorbed werewolf?"

Krosla," that might work, but sounds dangerous ... why not hit the citadel of light or briar hut village."

Ichary," be careful what you say to a blood drunk being."

Ichary is right to warn Krosla of the dangers the relic sphere, blood drunk beings especially human ones become uncontrollably violent and destructive over even the simplest of things.

Hartic and Caleb are explaining their presence at the assassins citadel. After long deliberation and chain of command they are let into the citadel of assassins. Now having been brought to where Qualis and Nexaug are, they have a talk about everything.

Qualis," yes your brother is here, but to no fault of ours he's been made a relic slave. The relics are bound to him as to control his action."

Caleb," like this?" shows the pyramid relics in the flesh of his hands.

Nexaug," no, the way yours are, you're a living relic relic wielder."

Qualis," if the eye were here, we could free the boy and obtain the relic diamond."

Hartic," relic diamond you say ... would that be the most expensive?"

Nexaug," yes, it unlocks the location to blueprints on how to make relics."

Hartic," then the eye for sixty-five percent of the profits, plus one-hundred geostones upfront."

Nexaug," thats excessive."

Qualis and Caleb," deal."

They awaken Sceiro who is handed the relic eye which seems to have a simplistic puzzle and a sequence of song tones required to activate it.

Raize had told Cirena to stay with the tome at the altar shrine on an instinctive notion. Which turned out to be wise as the new refortifications were in place upon his return, but the guards were enthralled in the midst of war with an onslaught of ghouls and werewolves which fought each other as well, so it was nothing but chaos. Raize commanded that the civilians and elders join Cirena at the altar shrine. Tredge, Vailez, and Raize would maintain holding the enemy back. During their fighting, onlookers Krosla and Ichary surmise machinations.

Krosla," well you get what you wanted, werewolves. But as a suggestion, give ghouls a shot first they're monsters that're smart but weaker than werewolves."

Ichary," thats not a bad idea, but I doubt ghouls have souls at least not normal ones … lets see."

She uses her relic to consume two guards and a ghoul by condensing them together and making one massive sphere of blood, then uses it to absorb it all cleanly. Then the two watch as the ghouls banshee is vampiritic and consumes the two guards' banshee.

Krosla," unique, I don't think I can control that one."

Ichary," well … right … lets see what a werewolf banshee does."

She rips apart a werewolf and absorbs, and two guards as well … the vamp banshee consumes the two guards banshee the werewolf banshee tears apart the vamp banshee … the spirits energy dies.

Krosla," the werewolf banshee I can command though."

Ichary," we have enough intel for now … the ghouls are leaving and the werewolves retreating."

The assassins citadel is facing an invasion of ghouls and vampires led by Lawrnev a vampire ghoul. He was caught by Irugez and a group of ghouls when he tried to leave the citadel of light. From the other side Sartoc infiltrates … the law mist from miswielding bloodletter is corrupting his intentions. After playing the song, right away the eye of convolution fuses into Sceiro's sternum. The very same moment Tikrah barges in.

Tikrah," undead invasion we're under attack."

Sceiro," I know!"

Sceiro flashs knowledge of how to wield the pyramid relics," go"

Caleb," yup … thats all cool, you and I gonna talk later though."

Qualis," do you know where the blueprints are, unlock the doors to their location?"

Sceiro looks up at the diamond labyrinth," its unlocked." pulls the relic disk shards collar off and reassembles the relic disk," you'll need this."

Nexaug," that's Hartic's job, Tikrah accompanies him. I'll head to a lookout post to make note of what's happening."

Sceiro heads to the battle, as Caleb spins the pyramids in reverse position and forces and immense energy wave into the ground creating an earthquake canyon chasm under the feet of a large number of ghouls and vampires … then he sends another wave to close the chasm crush burying them in one fell swoop. Sceiro gets to the edge of the assassins citadel and out imerges sartoc wrong wielding bloodletter. He strikes at Sceiro," hey," it pings off his bracers. Sartoc strikes again, this time the blades resonation hammer forces the bonds to break change, they become relic gauntlets that control environmental forces, terra nova gauntlet gloves. Caleb notices the trouble Sceiro is in and rushs to save him. But gets there too late, bloodletter is driven into his forehead, Sceiro dies insatantly. Caleb loses it … he uses pyramid point palm fires vibrational energy through Sartoc's head repeatedly. Sartoc appears to be dead, Caleb moves back to the ghoul vampire onslaught … he earthquakes a huge separation surround of the citadel. Picks up his brothers body and goes inside. Lawrnev sees sartocs body healing … so he takes bloodletterand is infused with the stored blood it has collected in battle, it doubles as a vampire blade, as such a vampire will gain blood knowledge by using it. Having won a trophy Lawrnev calls back his horde.

Hartic and Tikrah navigate their way through the diamond maze. They have a few close calls with traps and hit a few dead ends. They make it to a large door, open it, its a relic door. Inside there's a very large diamond, a map, and a relic diamond. Tikrah knowing Hartic's shifty ways grabs the map and diamond. Hartic touchs the relic diamond and the relic fuses into his head at the top.

Tikrah," really a damned thief is the inheriter of the assassins relic, fuck ever."

Hartic," we have to hurry, all the mazes are supposed to have relic disks placed where they belong before taking anything … or either you get trapped inside forever, or a blood relic ancient is resurrected to reign over people."

Blood Fluoretta," someone's a smartypants, lol."

Hartic," run."

Tikrah," no … I'll serve you if I can have any relic I want … deal?"

Fluoretta," you belong to me anyway silly ..." she blood infects Tikrah who drops the map and diamond, which Hartic grabs them quickly and leaves.

Caleb removes Sceiro's shirt ... notices the eye of convolution is emanating. He understands they're notes, plays them ... Sceiro's head heals and grows an extra eye thats ensymbolized, deep cut scars from the wound still remain. He opens his eyes," how bout a puffy puff."

Caleb," lol, I'm taking you home."

A werewolf rips to pieces, Krosla," how many does that make now?"

Ichary," fifty ... if you count the ten on the way here."

Krosla," that should be enough lets go."

Ichary," not with the way the guards of Briar Hut Village fight. They're over run with werewolves and if the ghouls return to add to their plight its over for them."

Krosla," why such concern?"

Ichary," keeping this area from unifying under one rule is fortuitus, the assassins already understand ... oldest small tribe is the correct ruling class. Things are ruled by bloodlines thats the plain and simple facts."

Krosla," so Briar Hut Village, why so special?"

Ichary," they're old law tribe in the wrong location. They use relic book rather than learn from it. They need a swift kick in the ass. The citadel of light should be their collective city state. If they don't fix things the dark legacy of their blood tribes will seize control."

Krosla," I don't suppose a dark bloodline in control is good for anyone."

Ichary," no, and with ghouls emerging, Briar Hut's dark bloodline ruler has already emerged."

Krosla," so save the village?"

Ichary," no, I don't know what legacy is what. Strip them of their book and use it to destroy the dark legacy that has arrived."

Vailez and Tredge rest a bit between waves of battle. They sent the soldiers to prep the woods edge with enflaments and dig pike pits before anything reachs the trench bridges.

Tredge," with all the traps and snares in place we'll beable to enslave some of these things ... wolfbeasts and ghouls."

Vailez's ears perk up at hearing this. He was raised old church relics cross crusader, which is to snuff out darkness no question no hesitation.

Vailez," what do you mean, this is a crusaders village right?"

Tredge," thats what the elders think ... Cirena, Raize and I decided to be dark spells crusader killers, its a better more profitable life."

Vailez," that can't be the only logic behind that decision, dark spells are enslaved by who they symbol slave."

Raize," under the right circumstances not so ... like if the symbol slave dies, which I'd be worried if he were here but Cirena and I realized Sceiro isn't the symbol slave, Caleb is."

Tredge," yeah, the one who believes the kid is birth marked that way."

Vailez," he's not."

Raize," nah, the village is actually supposed to rest elsewhere. Caleb is supposed to be a relic law destroyer and Sceiro is supposed to be a relic gatherer who wields a relic blade blood crusader weapon. Which I think is bullshit … should be my blade."

Vailez," wield it for what exactly?"

Tredge," purification of dark bloodline tribe, which includes us."

Vailez," then you're dark spell tribe?"

Raize," yeah, relic tome … dreamcatcher law."

Vailez," jeez … thats a relief … dreamcatcher law means you do the job the right way, using tribe law to earn the vision and keep track and make records. I'm relic cross crusader, its my job to make sure your work continues."

Tredge," but its relic power without a relic."

Vailez," which is necessary in forging new relics, and who knows … with everything going on Sceiro may be collecting relics as we speak."

Tredge," if thats true, Sceiro or Caleb will come to kill us one day."

Vailez," why … that doesn't make sense."

Tredge," because to bind someone as a symbol slave you have to be accountable for pain/loss in their life … their parents."

Vailez," you killed your own?"

Raize," no … this was their family hunting camp before Sceiro was born, they lived harsh on their own."

Vailez," so they stayed when you came or here by force."

Tredge," Caleb and his parents stayed … his older sister refused to end nomadic life."

An arrow hits its mark on an archer posts log with a scroll …

To: Briar Hut Village

From: Black Light City State formerly the Citadel of Light

Relic weapons were used there, by command of the black flame king … you are to deliver any and all relics of all kind and/or respond directly. You have two weeks to comply or war will be declared.

Notably your crown

Riscao the Dark

Raize looks at Tredge," go to the shrine she's to dark summon sacrifice the villagers for blood spell strength if the book is in danger of being claimed, and after that if it be so needed destroy the tome."

Tredge," right."

Hartic emerges to a Nexaug and Qualis waiting for him.

Hartic," we have to leave, there's a woken blood ancient … we need Caleb and Sceiro to forge new relic weapons if we're to survive."

But Fluoretta moves much faster than Hartic and was waiting in the shadows with them. Qualis being of no use was make into a living undead zombie like Tikrah …

Fluoretta," Nexaug join or die,"

As someone not stupid he joins. A fight is unavoidableNexaug kills Hartic … and then extracts the diamond relic and takes the diamond and map as well.

Fluoretta," good work lil puppy, now give here the relic."

He does and she fuses it into her chest between her breasts.

Fluoretta," clean this mess up ... those other two are very needed and I'd rather they stay calm and receptive. With this diamond which is a key and guided to the locations on the map, new relic weapons can be forged at an ancient foundry with the right materials."

She slips into the shadows, Tikrah drags Hartic's body away, Nexaug cleans up the blood. Caleb and Sceiro return to the inner part of the assassin's citadel. There Nexaug and Tikrah explain and lie to them everything they know.

Caleb," we're headed home, Sceiro has been in enough danger."

Tikrah," I understand that, but heading to your home is far more dangerous than locating the foundry which is in the opposite direction of what's turning into open war."

Nexaug," besides what can those gauntlet gloves of his do ... they were just bracers before."

Fluoretta, noticing that things won't work out unless she gets involved," those are controlling nature relic weapons. Sorry I don't mean to speak out of turn, I'm Fluoretta a symbolist historian."

Nexaug," well then with those he's like a god ... he's safe anywhere."

Tikrah," and with Caleb's pyramid relics he can force any and all enemies away."

Sceiro," we should still check on the rest of the villagers and Cirena."

Caleb," no ... they're right, besides our village might be under attack ... you go to the foundry with Nexaug,

I'll check on the village. We'll both take a few assassins as bodyguards ... cool?"

Sceiro," cool."

Irugez meets Lawrnev outside the throne room of the unlocked risen maze cube.

Lawrnev," what do you have to offer?"

Irugez," dymo relic, you?"

Lawrnev," bloodblade with blood."

They enter the throne room together. Seeing Riscao pacing in aggrevation, he sees their presence.

Riscao," for your sakes good news I hope."

Lawrnev," one fourth loss of infantry, one eighth increase of infantry ... and ..."

Riscao," one fourth loss ... explain."

Lawrnev," a magic user of some kind ... opened the ground itself and buried them deep underneath. Then carved out deep chasms between the citadel and enemy forces all the way around. Also there were werewolves."

Riscao," not bad competing with werewolves ... and if those ghouls are only buried they aren't lost, you had something else to say?"

Lawrnev," a trophy relic, its a blood blade."

Riscao," with blood condensed from fallen and wielders, I'll hold onto it ... and you?"

Irugez," ......" shuddering

Riscao," anything ... empty handed? At least a story fool, why spare your life."

Irugez," opened blood cube ... relic dymo ... plus knowledge of where the relic sphere is, very well guarded. Between wind chimes village and Briar Hut village."

Riscao," the sphere is powerful need relic cross or pyramid to wrench that away from it's wielder."

Lawrnev," someone with relic pyramid caused the losses at the assassins' citadel, the blood blade to get it," offering to mount an attack.

Riscao," not necessary, relic dymo is relic lawless … using it and the blood blade I'll make relic living undead, allowing me to turn my ghouls into pure blood vampire bloodline … an army most difficult to challenge even for the wielder of the relic sphere."

Caleb leads six others across the way back to his home, passing Wind Chimes Village which seems like a ghost town now. From there by pine valley river … where his group battled with bear clan beasts, who are human like monsters with the strength of four men, the speed of a deer, and claws harder than steel and sharper than the fins of a sunny. About halfway to his home his party rests at sugar maple lake. While there Caleb sees and ominous sight, a tormented spirit moves to the center of the lake where there is a small island and disapates. He goes to the island to investigate and finds a four pointed star relic … he's not sure what its for or what it does but knows it could be useful. After that he and his team make their way to and through the woods that lead to Briar Tunnel Rd where they will make their way to Caleb's village. At the entrance of Briar Tunnel Rd Caleb and his group come across Ichary and Krosla.

Caleb," hey Krosla you guys been doin okay?"

Krosla," sorry we don't have time for this."

Ichary," nor the patience or presence of witnesses."

Ichary fires lightening towards Caleb's men ... Caleb creates a barrier shield ... then uses his other hand to fire energy bullets at their feet and through the trees.

Caleb," I didn't start this fight now, I was being courteous."

Ichary," just gimme a clean shot, I'll be courteous dear."

Krosla," tell me where you're headed I promise to stay out of your way."

Caleb," Briar Hut, something tells me you were headed there yourselves."

Krosla," on the contrary just passing through, headed the other way in fact, a bit comical when you think of it, lol."

Caleb," we go our way, you go your way?"

Krosla," yea but you first mister energy shield."

Caleb," fair enough miss tuff," they enter Briar Tunnel Rd.

Krosla," we really staying away?"

Ichary," no, but this changes things, wanna watch'em a bit see whats what."

At the bridge Caleb encounters Tredge and a squad of men who detain them.

Caleb," what's this I live here dick."

Tredge," yea well war is upon us from the very place you and your brother were sent, we can't be too cautious. We're going to see Vailez.

Caleb," who is Vailez ... nah, fuck this."

Caleb force waves the guards and Tredge. Out jumps Raize swinging lightblade, not a sword made of light but a claymore made of highly dense stong metal but light as a feather ... its a minor relic blade. Whith it he sports a traditional shieldblade that the village produces. Caleb sensing dire consequences fires bullet point from both hands while avoiding lightblade's swing by staying in close quarters, punching holes in Raize's shieldblade. Raize swings hard this time after a few paces back for effectiveness. Caleb uses two energy shields to force grab the edge of the blade but its too chaotic to control that type of energy manipulation and creates a cut force that scores the blade in half. Cut half edged corner knicks Caleb, who then instinctively jumps back and earth shakes a divide between them all.

Caleb," we talk, as equals, peaceably ... or I leave ... deal?"

Raize and Tredge," deal

Raize," don't know how you did it but you're paying for my broken blade."

They all return to the village where Vailez is waiting.

Vailez," I see you've got a relic weapon ... were you sent here to support the citadels right to enforce war upon this place?"

Caleb," I'm from here, came to check on things ... if war is coming I'll fight. Not only that, Sceiro is traveling to a place where relic weapons are forged, we will have help."

Tredge," really."

Raize," to fix my light blade?"

Caleb," make a better one."

Vailez," with what you can do with those relics is good ... take him to Cirena, make sure he has all the instructions."

Sceiro and Fluoretta, who took Nexaugs place leaving him to run things back at the assassins citadel with Tikrah watching him closely. They have to pass through the canyon along the mountain river they call silver river. Its said never drink the water when its clear or silver, only when its red or white.

Fluoretta," the map says the foundry is inside the mountain, we just have to find the way in."

Sceiro," I already know ... I've been hit with alot of visions."

Fluoretta," does it have anything to do with that headband there used to be bandages, right?"

Sceiro," yea, the relic from my chest moved to where the wound is that took my life briefly." he takes off the headband, the relic has scar fused into the flesh and incorporates the original wound.

Fluoretta," hmm, permanent ... no one can take that from you except you maybe."

Sceiro," ... I can see everything don't know anything, its complicated."

Fluoretta," I understand that, things are complex."

Sceiro," lets just forget it."

Fluoretta," don't wanna tal ... shit."

A rushing flash flood brings an overflowing swollen river directly at the two's trail. Without thinking Sceiro forces earth to boulder rise as a barrier and forces the flow away and out of their way.

Sceiro," nope, I don't."

As they continue on out of the canyon, ahead of them a ways they would find themselves at cedarwood lake to the left are the trinity mountains. There are five mountains but three are three of the biggest in the world and are more or less equal give or take. They make and M shape facing Sceiro and Fluoretta, and a W away from them. It has another name … the five falls laws because they also make five waterfalls. When they get there the only thing left to do is find the way in.

Back at the Library of symbols the officials look for a solution to the chaos that is the citadel of light now. As Xertic and Zaqwa study the records, Xodah barges into the sanctuary.

Xodah," I think I found a possible solution but its a long shot and very difficult."

Zaqwa," that makes sense, speak."

Xodah," according to this scroll there's a place to enact a mechanism that will allow the original city state to return from being lowered into the ground. It may not change what has risen but maybe it can turn people back to regular people instead of living as ghouls and such.

Xertic," not until we know for sure … too much wrong has occured by our incorrect assumptions."

Xodah," but its simple and in light of the predicament that is the present, there's not much left at stake."

Xertic," enough I said no."

Xodah,' except our lives'

Nexaug speaks with his bishops and high knights. He tells them they are to test a new toxic tip poison on lower ranking assassins to inspect its effectiveness and usefulness. They are told to have their high crows perform the task and report back to them in a week and a half. After two weeks there seems to be cases of distopia, as in vomiting, diarhea, and fever. The toxic tip is listed as a self innoculative biotech weapon toxic art. Thusly it is cleared for use by half of the citystate of assassins. A special classification of no high ranks to recieve the designed vaccines as is it is still label listed as experimental possible danger risk.

Xodah takes it upon himself to trigger the citadels return mechanism. According to the scroll and map its not that far into the maze cube. Which is easy enough to get into. After he makes it inside, he traverses the corridors. After he makes it through the task of reaching the mechanism he initiates it … he hears alot of rumbling noise. It must've worked, something worked.

Riscao," lol, who would be so kind as to give me access to the rest of the citizens of the city state that remain in their citadels, hahaha."

Xodah," no," he moves to reverse the switch … Riscao is facing him.

Riscao," you're too intelligent to even turn let alone leave alive."

Riscao opens Xodah's head and pulls out his brain and consumes it. Its not even a battle when the dark city state's forces meet the remaining survived of the city state of light. Half made into ghouls and vampire and half left as blood farming stock.

Tredge takes Caleb to Cirena. At the shrine Cirena leads the villagers in a tribal thought. After Caleb and Tredge have a word with Cirena.

Cirena," I can understand you with those new weapons ... but lil Sceiro has things like that?"

Caleb," its a long story, I won't deprive him of telling it."

Ichary forces hail to fall down as Krosla uses her relic charm to send slave banshees to attack the three of them. Tredge moves straight into dual shieldblade position, Caleb already barriering them all from the hail and fires energy bullets. Ccirena fires about seven arrows from a light recurve bow, everything moves through the banshees. Cirena loses her bow and opens the book ... uses incantation demonic dreamcatcher, that traps the banshees in a pentagram that they are pulled into by a vortex spell. Ichary and Krosla flee having lost twelve banshees.

Tredge," is there no fuckin downtime anymore."

Caleb," what was that?"

Tredge," don't Cirena."

Cirena," he needs to know about the book."

Caleb," book?"

Cirena," its a relic, a book of magic spells ... but I have to use it sparringly, there are costs to using much of it."

Caleb," have you always had that?"

Cirena," grew up learning it, where is he?"

Caleb," on his way to build relic weapons."

Fluoretta," we're never gonna find the door."

Sceiro," maybe the door has a curtain."

Fluoretta," a what ... shit, which one? Can those mitts of yours lift these curtains?"

Sceiro tries, the water of the falls is too heavy ... its easier to add a step barrier at the top parting the falls in two. So one by one til all five are open falls. The falls each have their own unique way inside the mountains.

Fluoretta," so the foundry is all five mountains and falls."

As they make their way into the mountains, the both look for torchs. In the meantime Sceiro's glove makes a flame of light for now. Fluoretta notices an oil trough along the wall. They light it lighting the path all the way down through the corridors. In the foundry they find basic instructions for making relic weapons. The process involves first physically forging the construct normally by hand using a hammer and anvil. After the construct is made perfect by the smith it must be etched with runic signature. Then the construct must be melted down after all normal final tempering and edging if needed. While in its second smelted state the relic smith must add his/her own or the recipients blood to quench the construct with will law and speaking the runic signature message as 'written law prewritten that which is spoken'. Doing so will cause the construct to reform. Then its required to etch the construct with a name stain the etching with bloodline, thusly giving bloodline legacy the right to alter the construct the power to do so ... which is based on smith, blood inheriter, and user. As the construct relic is of a self conscious entity that develops a will of its own.

Fluoretta," jeez this is vicious stuff, you up for this ... I'm not up for this."

Sceiro," its and exaggeration of the truth, if you made a sword one person wouldn't have enough blood to quench it. Only if you wanted or needed to make a really strong one would you have to completely quench it. So you'd have multiple people to bleed for it … which must be where bloodline right comes in, alternating ownership."

Fluoretta," you think? Nah you know and I know you know I'm dangerous."

Sceiro," yea I figured I'd die on this trip."

Fluoretta," not til after you help me make a new relic of ancient relics. I didn't get to my sphere my enemy did. Its help me or I carve out the one in your skull and make due. Besides its easy for you with those gloves, precious lil mitts they are."

Sceiro," a sphere, it has to be more complex than that?"

Fluoretta," a lil. A smelted titanium sphere inscripted 'orb of law life', hammer smelt quenched with a same size sphere of my blood, re-inscripted 'law orb of cosmic'.

Sceiro," sounds simple actually."

The assassins fortress barrier is endanger of being overrun, with the issues of a three front war. Werewolves on one side, vampires and ghouls on the other, and a zombie outbreak to boot. Not to mention the werewolves seem to have a leader now … Oxgruf a redhaired wolf pushing against the assassins and the vampires. The assassin elder bishops and devout knights blame Nexaug as they collect all of the most important records and dealings. An agreement of a massive bounty on Nexaugs head is placed. As the battle rages on, due to the severe reality of what Tikrah's infection is, Nexaug decides to quarter and behead him. And then orders his remaining assassins to do as such in the battle.

The same time the assassins are being attacked Briar Hut is at war with Tredge, Raize, and Caleb defending with guards as best they can. Krosla and Ichary are also there taking advantage of the opportunity to get rid of Caleb and claim his relics and get closer to the relic tome.

Tredge," you two go protect Cirena, three relic users together can comeback and do more than stifle this shit."

Caleb," you sure."

Raize," he;s right."

Ichary," lets go I want that relic user put down."

Halfway to the shrine krosla cuts off raize with a heavy relic ringed fist knocking him down."

Caleb," raize!"

Raize," keep going I got this."

About two miles from Cirena, Ichary emerges in Calebs path.

Ichary," no more games."

Ichary forces trees to the ground ripping up roots. Caleb creates energy bursts sending them away. Ichary soars a broken branch punching a hole through caleb's chest. Due to all the commotion Cirena decides to bind herself to the tome, putting on a self made slave collar. An infinite wellspring of knowledge is granted to her, the book is hers she is the book. Ichary gets to the shrine to see Cirena with a slave collar chaining her to the relic tome. Ichary slyly sneaks away, not wanting a fight with what looks like a relic god. Meanwhile raize who was knocked to the ground ... luckily his blade was cut down making for a quicker stabbing killing strike disbatching Krosla easily. Seeing the value of her rings raize takes them and they slide on his fingers.

Raize," my relic rings now."

And back at the battle, though no relics were being used ... Tredge fought vailiantly with dual shieldblades against onslaught after onslaught of vampire, ghoul, and werewolf. So much enemy blood spilled before he was felled, no one will deny the stains in that field and who left them, and also consider the weapon used as a relic weapon.

Before Sceiro makes Fluoretta's sphere, he chooses to make something else first. He decides a triangle should be simple enough. He follows the process, inscribes it with 'equal law', then continues the process, it becomes a solid pyramid with tribal symbols. Confused but shrugs it off and re-inscribes it with 'law thar is justified'. It fuses into his right hand, pyramid cell tech takes over, tapping the power of the eye of convolution and allows him to make her sphere with ease.

Fluoretta," thats a god relic you just made ... wanna trade,"(shakily)

Sceiro," nope, now you can't kill me. Try it I gave it a name, 'core sphere'."

Fluoretta activates it, dark crescent bracelets bind to her arms," these are stronger than my originals."

Sceiro," make any others or head back?"

Fluoretta," need their blood to make them, head back ... I have someone to kill, you?"

Sceiro," wanna help my village so we'll part halfway."

Fluoretta," k"

The assassins left under Nexaug's authority beat back the invading hordes and sorted out and dealt with their living undead by keeping them as outdoor perimeter guard dogs. Nexaug openly blames the elder bishops and devout knights that left, accountable. Most agree as they were the signature orders. Now Nexaug petitions hisfellow assassins to take the fight to the enemy, or if there is a better way to do things to come forward. It is the largest army the assassins have evr massed. Their war strategy is to play on their strengths, using gorilla warfare tactics. So in separate directions and groups do they march. Like interlopers on a mission.

Fluoretta and Sceiro come to thirteen points road.

Fluoretta," yea, sure you don't wanna come give me a helping hand?"

Sceiro," you've got plenty of juice you'll be fine."

Fluoretta heads out of sight, Sceiro raises his right hand and creates a hole in reality ... walks through it. He then emerges at Briar Hut with bodies upon the soil everywhere ... werewolves eating carcauses. He blows them up into parts. Sees Tredge's dead body, or so he thought.

Tredge," kid what are you doing here."

Sceiro," what happened here, where's Caleb, Cirena, everyone?"

Tredge," not much time left ... if they're still alive, that way towards the shrine ... past the graveyard."

Tredge passes on. Sceiro places some herb in Tredges mouth and puffs a pipe a few before moving on. He then treks through past the cemetary and reachs the torn down trees where he sees his brother Caleb's body ... mangled and limp on the post. He wants to cry but can't, he finds himself in a sort of shock. Being bound to the relic tome and Sceiro was her bond slave, his distress causes the book to drag her to him. When she gets there, she can't help but tear up and wrap her arms around the poor kid.

Amidst the battles and explosions of the assassins chaotic reprisal for overbearance, Fluoretta contemplates how to move to the leader Riscao who is a blood ancient she must take down. Then in a separate location through a three dimensional pyramid portal emerge Sceiro and Cirena there seeking vengence. Fluoretta makes her way to the law throne, when she gets there she sees Riscao sitting in wait, highly vexed. Before she moves down there Ichary happens behind her."

Ichary," that looks like mine give it here."

Fluoretta," wait!" she doesn't, and hurls a massive rock at her, which knocks her down at Riscao's feet.

Riscao," well a demigod relic ..." swiftly grabs a blade and drives it into her heart, takes the relic for himself.

Ichary hides, hesitant after witnessing that. Sceiro and Cirena arrive.

Sceiro," my brother's dead because of you."

Riscao," really you think so?"

Ichary jumps down," do you know that's mine?"

Cirena," I can send you from whence you came."

Riscao," then do so, cause I used to be Caleb, but I died ... tree slam right."

Ichary," you don't look much better sorry about that."

Riscao," don't mention it."

Cirena," so what go back to stop yourself from dieing?"

Riscao," you know I hadn't thought of that, do you think it'd work? No, I just want to stay out of hell and do everything I'm supposed to to not feel pain."

Sceiro," hell isn't real."

Riscao," oh but it is ... traveling through bloodline legacy improperly is endless suffering, don't speak of what you don't know boy. I notice your lil black book ... maybe you are the one to end this all and free me from my painful bonds."

Cirena," if it ends the bloodshed fine."

After studying her book for some time, there's nothing but imprisonment spells that require a god relic ... which Sceiro explained his earlier,

Cirena," here we are, this'll turn you back into a regular Caleb," they cast the spell and imprison him inside himself as a demon construct relic. Ichary wastes no time for conversation and leaves. Cirena decides to care for Sceiro and the two go back to the village.

When Ichary slinked away after the final ordeal with Riscao, she made sure to go back and snatch the demon construct he was sealed in. that was five years ago. Ichary being very educated on the relics since then, sought Calebs place of death. Which was not easy, as he died bound with relics which cause the wielder to bleed until said time as which the relics are consumed. This causes strange living wilderness though reclusive, very dangerous to traverse. It's like a living tombthat demands respect for that which has passed on. And so for three years she has battled and sneaked her way through the ever changing new forest of confusion, where all who live near it stay away. Finally she makes it to Calebs resting place. The stump protruding from his chest out his back into the ground, driven like a stake from how she flung it into him. Blue vines growing from his wound, feeding the forest. And so she carefully approaches holding up the demon construct which halts the vines and forest's controlling assault she was unaware of.

Ichary utters," that which you are, return to what you once were to claim what you might;ve been."

And so Caleb's eyes peer open with yellow light shining from them. The vines become red briar with black tipped thorns, that reach out wrapping around the construct like a knotted ball of bramble ... pulls him off of the tree stake and the demon construct is placed in his chest as it heals. Also what appears to be Fiscao emerges from Calebs body with the pyramid relics that were Calebs and still having the crescent sphere bracelets he took from Fluoretta. The demon construct stays in Calebs chest, his body wrapped in red briar black thorns.

Ichary," riscao!?"

"no, hahaha ... he's gone, I'm Cisaro and he's no longer Caleb."

Caleb," yes I am ... ergh!"

Cisaro," oh the partial consumption of relics in your blood seem to stave off your change ... how interesting."

Ichary who retreated behind a tree watchs everything. Caleb's eyes go yellow again and he moves briar vines to wrap around Cisaro's hand, it pulls out one of the pyramid relics. Cisaro lets out blood curdling screams. Calebs briar vine body consumes the pyramid, it disintegrates. Cisaro uses his other hand to fire a blast to knock Caleb away, then the forest springs violently to life. Cisaro flees. Ichary screams," wait not trying to hurt you!" The forest doesn't stop even though Caleb does," run." she listens,"sorry!" She fires a wave of energy down to skyrocket her up and out of the forest. The briar vines nearly catch her when Caleb emerges building a wall of his own briars. She sails away in escape, he falls back into the forest.

Raize and his infantry are bottlenecked at the western bridge by ghouls.

Raize," should've had Cirena send bow men."

Sceiro fifteen now dismounts a clidesdale with a flip and enters the fray.

Raize," use those gauntlets make light work of this boy."

Sceiro," where's the fun in that," now brash in his coming of age, as he sports a double sided flail staff braining ghouls mercilously.

Raize," damn it boy you're gonna drive me to drink, at least one side we're surrounded."

Sceiro," earth walls work for ya," he builds stone walls on each side of the bridge.

Raize," yea thats great, but I'm curious why things gotta be so difficult."

Sceiro," Cirena said you're gettin fat old man."

They finish off the ghouls.

Raize," she did't really say that did she … I mean."

Sceiro," nah thats my opinion, she said you've been restless and agitated … lol."

Raize," you're too mean …"

Sceiro," what I know you like a challenge."

Raize," I also like a sure thing and …"

Sceiro," yea with me its always a sure thing … but it won't always."

Raize," you talking bout your brother again … not your fault lil man couldn't be helped."

Sceiro (whispers)," its … lets get back, your men can help with the trophies I baged before I heard you needed saving."

Back at Iron Shrine Village which is now where Briar Hut Village maintains safe boarders, Cirena just finished a sermon when Raize and Sceiro return.

Cirena," good to see you both ok, despite the recklessness of you two."

Raize," so you heard of the overzealous nature of this one … lol."

Cirena," I did and am not happy, he's been raised better than that … I hold you accountable for his brash nature."

Sceiro," I;m fine I'd never do anything too foolish you know that."

Raize," besides I think it was a good assessment of his capabilities … to run things here while I take enough men to that relic foundry and we finally muster the relic arsenal we need, then it can become a business after we safen our territory."

Cirena," I think I can manage home alone, his gauntlets would make that process easier with his geo abilities, he could forge and smelt metals for your weapon smithing."

Raize," I suppose, I just worry bout the other villags who have joined our flock, how much can they be trusted."

Sceiro," Cirena has a large enough group of followers to keep the peace and maintain control … and worse comes to worse her tome is more than powerful enough to command respect from the other villages. Plus with ghoul packs and werewolf tribes around, people would rather rely on people ... we're not hte assassins, nor the denizens of the city state of darkness and light."

Raize," good point, ruled by vampires they are, and the assassins are plagued by zombies and disease ... they've become poison addicts just to survive."

Cirena," beside I've copied relic symbols from the book for you to inscribe upon the weapons you make to ensure their quality."

Sceiro," so when do we leave?"

Meanwhile Lawrnev sits upon the throne in the city state of darkness and light, in charge of whats now an entire city state of vampire with the relic weapon bloodletter at his disposal.

Lawrnev," its been five years, where is my dymo ... the blood slaves will not last as the ghoul populace grows. With the dymo I can continuously turn sired human slaves from ghoul to vampire. Capturing werewolves for their unique ghoul transforming flesh is too difficult on a large scale."

Stayne," we've searched everywhere the master has ever been. Strangely the area is too great to cover with our manpower."

Lawrnev," how do you mean, explain."

Tarn," its as if he lived in two places at the same time, his scent his blood has been too vast in travels."

Stayne," and there's a place strong with his scent, a forest that has claimed most of the lives of our men sent there."

Lawrnev," then burn the forest you speak of. If that isn't where he's hiding or died then its where he has ruled from last."

The intelligent red haired werewolf known as Oxgruf along with his elite self turned tribe sit by a fire eating elk they hunted down, wary to keep an open ear out for hungary wolverine. The only pack animals capable of bringing them down. And they happen to be interupted by a falling Ichary, who was sensed coming by only Oxgruf who is familiar with her scent. Frozen in fear for landing in the center of a werewolf pack Ichary trembles.

Ichary (whispers)," shit."

Oxgruf," hold."

Ichary even more petrified at the fact that they speak," dear god I'm fucked," she thinks.

Oxgruf," no need to fret dear love, I may look different but I still remember that tipped whip of yours … that was mean by the way … meaner that you had rummaged my pockets all that time ago."

Ichary (gasps)," … ah, ah, oxgruf?!"

Oxgruf," in the fur, lol."

Ichary," you look different … ch … ch … changed you have."

Oxgruf," don't be frightened, though you were mean, I remember your trade and am in need of a friend."

Ichary," haha, weapons for wolf people … I dare say twould be a sight to see, but I am far from my station if me wagon is still there."

Oxgruf," by Tree Cove Village, it is … half the village mindless wolf beasts, the other half my tribe."

Ichary," I could use food stores and some rest as payment, my other plans have fallen to disarray ... oh yes and no biting or scratching me, I'll not be one of your tribe."

Oxgruf," sounds fair have some elk."

Nexaug had new war bishops appointed that weren't zombie infected. The zombies were beaten back out of the assassins stronghold but can't be killed unless dismembered and burned to ash. And the ghouls Caleb had buried became infected by zombie infection when it rained on the ash and gave rise to a weaker group of half vampire. But they look like healthy people, not long fanged unnatural skinned beings, who late in the night four years ago scattered to small groups of twenty, about ten groups, to build their own small kingdoms. Two of the groups returned to join the assassins as guards. And so now after four years of vampire assault upon the lower ranked assassins being turned, there is a division between the vampire assassins and the poison addicted ruling class. Who can't be turned because of the causticity in their blood. And the one who gained control of the assassins and brought them from the brink of destruction, Nexaug was neither ruling class assassin but also can't be turned as long as he uses both poison and toxic vaccines on a regular basis. Because of this the tribes of half vampires have taken over the stronghold, though are still opposed to traditional full blooded vampires.

Tristena," haha, who wants to take bets on how long that Nexaug can stay on his feet?"

Dresdin," how mean of you ... in by the way, lol."

Barqua," I'll join."

Dresdin," thought you were against gambling?"

Barqua," I am, but his resolve is commendable ... a real testament to the assassins dedication, i like making notes, this'll help me stay attentive."

Tristena," great I'll get a pool going and get back to ya guys."

Barqua," hey this thing needs rules for posterity."

Tristena," rules, you're no fun."

Dresdin," he's right, someone might slip him too much poison to win and then he's dead funs over and our ambassador is gone."

Barqua," not only that, I'm taking scientific notes ... no altering his process."

Tristena," oh, when you guys put it that way, tah tah."

Barqua," I mean it bitch."

Dresdin," dude don't call her a bitch, lol."

Barqua," fuck up ... bitch."

Navwec an assassin crow rank mixes poison in a mortar and pestal as the clergy discuss the issues that plague them.

Zarlo," these half blood vampires, their affliction is unique and if harnessed can be a highly valuable commodity."

Feng," yes but our poison blood makes it unusable to us, so how much of a commodity is it, only a benefit to our future generations."

Mainge," unless we can better the benefits they will always control it."

All sit quietly for a moment.

Renge," you so busy, what say you, any ideas?"

Navwec," well our ambassador Nexaug ..."

Renge," what of him?"

Navwec," it seems with the right combination of poisons and toxins, the blight is stoppable maybe even reversable … maybe not Nexaug but another or other candidates to be trained as specific toxic and poison regimented assassins who are used to contract the vampirism bridging the gap to enable the blight to evolve to be useful to the presently immune bloodlines."

Feng," if that's the plan then our work has already begun, using Nexaug's evolving blight will be used to bridge the gap. Injection of his blood to lower rank immune to begin as soon as possible."

Renge," see that the order is given Navwec, you are now in charge of the relayance of information on the matter."

Navwec," yes sir."

Sceiro and Raize along with Vailez, accompanied by a hundred soldiers, find themselves about halfway to five falls laws foundry. The men bring smithing tools and as much metals as can be brought. Finding out on this trip that Vailez is relics cross crusader, Sceiro is interested in his own relics and understanding them.

Sceiro," do you know anything about this," removing his headband to reveal the eye of convolution.

Vailez," the eye, its said it drives the wielder insane with visions chaotic."

Raize," maybe a sane individual but Sceiro is as crazy as they come, lol."

Sceiro," I get flashes of knowledge and of things to come, I just don't know if they're true … with a name like eye of convolution."

Vailez," they call it that because no one's been said to have endured its power ... it may be different for you, no one as young as you has ever used it to my knowledge."

Raize," maybe he's just strong bloodline, or lacks the madness of age to become afflicted."

Sceiro," and this," removing his glove and reveals the pyramid god relic he forged.

Vailez," thats new, from the way it interacts with your flesh, that's a deity relic, where?"

Sceiro," it was at the foundry left behind I suppose," his lies to hide his forging.

Vailez," I wonder with a proper combing what might be found. But it may be fortunate of you, that may be why you have focus with the eye."

Raize," don't worry soon enough we will have an arsenal of relic weapons to use and sell, sell the weaker ones anyway, lol."

In the heart of the Forest of Confusion Caleb battles his innermost demons.

Belac,' give in to me, I've brought you this far let me win.'

Caleb," no, who are you, can you hear me."

Belac,' yes, listen to me I can help you ... but I need to be in control.'

Labec,' no, he lies he wants to steal your life.'

Caleb," what, who are you."

Voices starting as whispers that grow into shouts then deafening noise agonise Caleb. He passes out. Hours pass by before he awakens, there's a message in the dirt.

[I am Iabec the other is Belac, you can not trust Belac, but I am now too weak to help you, other than leave you messages in the sand or on paper if handy, good luck]

Worried of Belac discovering the message, Caleb scuffs his feet over the dirt.

Caleb," Cirena and her book may help me, I must find her as soon as possible."

Cisaro watchs as pureblood vampires work to set the Forest of Confusion ablaze. Seeing that they are led by his former generals he decides to act.

Salvic," poor oil at the bases of the trees next to the powder kegs and make sure to stick clay tech on the really big ones."

Cisaro," is this where we left you working five years ago?"

Salvic," lord my king, is that you … you don't look like yourself. We have orders to capture or kill you."

Cisaro," and whom do you have greater faith in?"

Salvic," others may disagree, but you sire."

Cisaro," then return me to my seat, for the five years away I discovered where to make such weapons and with what is unleashed they are needed."

Salvic," but how?"

A lower rank eavesdropping hungry for a rise in position chimes in.

Torrin," as a new member, he does look different it would be easy to return him and challenge Lawrnev for the throne."

Salvic," we need more than a challenge with his relic blade handy … we need dissention and cudetah."

Cisaro," then use time to our advantage … the beast thats loose a relic blade will not save him. And when this attack on the living forest turns rye, we will have ranks of dissent."

Torrin," living forest?"

Salvic," yes, I've been expecting disaster here. You Torrin pick well trusted and stay clear away from the events that unfold."

And events did unfold, the forest pushed sugar into the boarders to be ignited to cause the trees to produce a massive amount of alcohol in the roots that streched under the feet of the men who set the blaze. Such ill fated events with the forest that grew back twice as thick affected morale, which is now a perfect breeding ground for dissention. Salvic, Torrin, and Cisaro had no issue recruiting against the ill rule of Lawrnev.

Oxgruf and his pack brought Ichary back to her wagon just beyond Tree Cove Village. Then he sent his pack to the village to retrieve as many of the villages weapons and armor for reforging. Meanwhile Oxgruf assisted her in her shield making.

Ichary," we can make ten oversized leather wooden shields for you and your men, that enough?"

Oxgruf," not nearly, my whole pack is seven-hundred strong. Half are women and we are breeding, the one thing that separates us from full blooded werewolves and vampires."

Ichary," with that many forge for yourselves."

Oxgruf," that's why you're needed love, I need you to forge smithing tools big enough for us to use and to teach us how."

Ichary," normally I'd say for the right price deary, but in the aire of the world ... keep me fed, well clothed and protected and no turning me rule not get violated and we're in business, what do you say?"

Oxgruf," deal, for now first thing's first the weapons we need to stay safe."

Ichary and Oxgruf with his small group work through the week to melt down the supplies from the village. Then Ichary spends the next two weeks making large weapons with her little forge and instructs the group to smoke the animal hydes they have into leather to make armor, because of the half werewolves' size leather armor is most sensable. After those two weeks with well made shields and blades they embark towards wolfclaw lakes where Oxgruf's kind thought fitting to make settlement.

As Caleb sneaks his way through the village making his way to find Cirena, Belac toys with his mind.

Belac,' why are we here, that pyramid we've tasted was only half the relic ... or do you crave the taste of blood now?'

Caleb," shut up ... you need to just die."

Belac,' I'm game ... open one of our veins, lol.'

Caleb," go to hell you're not gonna beat me."

Belac,' relax I already know we can't die from just any wound, besides the scent of a relic is here.'

Cloaked fire mages notice Calebs presence and scatter ... alerting defensive trappers who after the mages toss flash incendiaries, throw multiple bolas to tie and subdue Caleb ... who not wanting a fight refuses to easily break the bindings. When the guards understand who they've captured they are highly confused and surprised to see Caleb after such a long time and word that he was dead. Without hesitation though they take him to the prison and report to Cirena of their discovery.

As Raize, Vailez, and Sceiro with their entourage are encamped and keeping cozy by the fire a group of people come to see if they can join the fire sit, which by that phrase means a request to talk. Raize and Vailez agree, Sceiro weary from travel retires to bed away from earshot.

Raize," whats on your mind friends?"

Zaila," we have a proposition for you and your men."

Vailez," which would happen to be?"

Korint," well we are a group of half vampires, we're not immortal lest we feed enough intelligently, but that's easy cuz we are stronger than our human selves."

Vailez," and you're looking for work?"

Raize," or trade?"

Zaila (smiling)," both ... its easy to turn others and we can stay young on the blood of livestock without killing it til it's time to eat it, and in turn I could use a boyfriend, hehe."

Korint," Zails ... c'mon, anyway we are strong in the day and night, we just need steady stable village life, or ..."

Vailez," or you'll die eventually."

Zaila," right."

Raize," I'll leave the decision to my friend, but personally I like the idea of immortality without a real drawback."

Vailez," if that's a statement because of my status don't worry, I'm on board … I feel the same way."

Korint," your men too?"

Vailez," Sceiro?"

Raize," not all of them … select ones, and yea he needs something to anchor him he's getting restless."

Zaila," no … you're not gonna tell him he doesn't get turned … we're peacefulish."

Vailez," understandable."

Raize, "mhm," 'we'll see'

Nexaug having just been held down for a series of blood injections by a special group of assassins and half bloods, neither side knowing the other's intentions but don't fight specifically to not break the peace accord, stumbles into the kitchen and grinds black pepper and packs a pipe with it, as smoking some spices is poisonous. He continues his fight to stay independent and strong especially because he's confused as to whether the assassins are trying to help or not.

Tarloc," see look he's on his ass, who had full moon's second day?"

Tristena slinks in," damn it … I don't know about your side bets ladies but Dresdin wins the first pool. Ninty fucking ring stones." She pulls out leaf rolls, lights one, (to Nexaug)," I know you're busy working sweetie but care for a break, I'm sure medicinal shock might give you a helping hand. Or does puppet wanna give in and be my lil toy toy, lol?"

Nexaug," fu … fu … fuck off beauty," he snatchs the smoke," tha … ha … anks."

Tristena pouts and kisses his forehead, blows a puff in his face," humph, if its like that, tah tah … try not to stumble again til half moons third day and I'll see you get more smokes."

Nexaug," hm."

Tarloc," hey that's cheating."

Nexaug," technically its just incentive which from you is degrading," he winks at her as he weezes and chokes on his pepper pipe and leaf roll.

Tarn updates Lawrnev of their progress on werewolf flesh stocked for ghoul turning … the earlier a ghoul is turned the stronger the vampire starts, which is important for their work. Meanwhile Stayne waits around the corner in fear for the bad news of the forest disaster having gotten reports from scouts.

Tarn," we have four-hundred pounds of werewolf meat left sir, but one was taken down last week."

Lawrnev," is that all … correct me if I'm wrong but that would make roughly seven-hundred pounds of ghoul transforming meat?"

Tarn," ye … ye … yes."

Lawrnev," then tell me how our work can continue when it takes the feasting of about a hundred pounds of werewolf flesh to make a blood drinker!"

Tarn," I don't know … hunting werewolves is difficult, we have to trap large enough game just to kill one … if we can, they're strong."

Lawrnev," of course they're strong, thats why their flesh works so well. A city of warriors and legislators but none seem to be hunters how appauling. Tell me someone has some idea how to rectify our problem."

Mairlexa," I have a perfect plan sire."

Lawrnev," speak, lets hear this perfect plan."

Mairlexa," reserve the rest of our stock of meat for a time."

Lawrnev," and let ghouls decay, for what purpose you daft bitch?"

Mairlexa," to find and turn specific people we identify as skilled hunters."

Lawrnev," my dear that is an intelligent remedy to our issue … come taste knowledge from bloodletter."

As such being Lawrnev's drug reward he bestows on those deemed worthy.

Lawrnev," now bring forth Stayne, I'd like to hear of more good work."

Stayne grabs the reporting scout," you're telling him not me."

Lawrnev," so you've brought a friend how quaint … explain to me the good news, or is it bad?"

Stayne shoves the scout forward," you're report," he barks.

Scout," the company on it's way to return … minor losses no success, though losses were still substantial. And from the reports low morale and the forest not only regrew but designed a countermeasure to the attack."

Lawrnev," I see, so I'm expected to lower morale further by punishing the reporting scout Stayne? For your failure to adequately delegate and delineate in an effective proper fashion?"

Stayne," sire I made adequately clear the fact that the forest itself were/is a cognitively living. With your permission I'd like authority to make example of those in charge of the returning company."

Lawrnev," I see, so you do know what you're doing as an authoritative position requires. Then start boosting morale by appropriating the punitive action that should be taken upon yourself for not shouldering responsability directly as a good commander should."

Stayne protests," I highly think such action so excessive not be necessary."

Lawrnev," and scout you … whats your name, what say you?"

Scout," my name is Skarlo, and in my opinion he deserves punitive action, ten lashs at least … that I am more than willing to do my part in …"

Stayne," shut it you bitch of a dog!"

Lawrnev," no you shut it … continue your statement I'm interested."

Skarlo," I would've said more than willing to shoulder or deliver, my aim isn't to rule … but bitch of a dog, I'll shoulder and deliver."

Stayne gasps and then falls silent, as the court laughs with Lawrnev smiling.

Lawrnev," shoulder and deliver how lively … and so shall it be, and when after whoever remains standing in a lash for lash will be my new commander. And the other, well I suppose that depends on my assessment of the winners conviction, lol."

And so a lash for lash duel commenced, each taking their turn tasting a lick of a whip. After the ninth lash

Stayne collapsed, Skarlo though weak stood at eight and turned to a court guard.

Skarlo," I'm minus two lashes and that one is incapable ... you mind?" offering the whip as he kept in mind what Lawrnev said.

Lawrnev," willful conviction stands, another lash is not necessary. I expect good things from you Skarlo ... be sure to drink your fill and heal, that one gets half rations he doesn't deserve to heal quickly."

Raize and Vailez discussed with Zaila and Korint that turning them should wait til after they forge new weapons because they were headed to the relic foundry. They agreed needing no further explanation, forging weapons is no easy task. Also they were asked to make weapons too ... as vampire relic weapons can be made by vampires bloodline then half vampires might be able to make both or something in between. Now upon rethinking things after a few days Vailez asked Zaila and Korint to change him into a halfblood, not wanting to wait as his profession that was so dangerous never afforded him such opportunity, he wished it not to slip through his fingers. When they arrived at five mountains five falls, Raize told Vailez who knew his decision, to spike Sceiro's food and drink with vampire blood. They had decided to set up camp outside the foundry and bring the materials inside in shifts to keep the forge process secret. Which is when that night they made camp was when Sceiro's dinner was readied. And Sceiro ate and drank heartily that night ... and also dabbled in his hunter's remedies much like his brother Caleb used to. Whether Sceiro would become a halfblood remains to be seen.

The next day Sceiro was busy mixing metals for weapon forging while the metals already ready were worked into blades. Korint, Zaila, and Vailez made rapiers for speedy striking, and they discovered that halfbloods relic weapons are different than normal relic blades, for instance the blades themselves are bloodthirsty and absorb the blood of the fallen to them. Also much like bloodletter they pass knowledge from the blood collected to the weilder. The vampire blades are blue and crave blood like vampires do, also the vampire blades are very cold and highly ridged. Raize still human, reforged lightblade and so his claymore is newly forged and takes on characteristics of him, also lightblade remains hot when striking an enemy yet cool to the touch to the weilder. Sceiro produces many arrowheads that come out purple and seem to attract the vampire blades as it seems the arrowheads are living blood weapons. The rest of their men continue the process as specific groups of them are made into halfbloods to forge new vampire weapons and armor. Though Raize waits as the vampire blades make him hesitant assuming becoming a vampire may have drawbacks he hadn't considered. So Raize works with the men on building normal relic blades, mostly sheildblades as is their village's mainstay go to weapon. Sceiro also makes a relic bow and a staff double flail. Then he forges something Cirena requested him to make, a metal pocket watch relic with her blood, and he curious as he was made one of his own,

Cirena eager to investigate this alive Caleb goes to the prison where he sits in wait.

Cirena," how is it possible you're alive?"

Caleb," I don't know but I need Your help, I'm plagued by madness and think your book may be the only thing that can aid me."

Caleb's body jutts out a secound head made of the demon relic and begins to speak," oh that won't happen, Caleb must serve as my vessel," All the while Caleb screams ins agony til he passes out and turns out is Belac who takes over and not peaceable enough to stay in his prison cell. Ripping apart the bars as he portends his desires," that book though I sense is a relic … I must eat it, it must belong to me … give it here girl!"

Cirena," never, this relic is a part of me you'll never have it."

Even though Belac touched it and ate half of the cover, Cirena summons a spell of infinite protection around herself, making Belac furious with rage as he mercilessly attacks Cirena's spell sheild to no avail. Then Cirena's guards knock out Belac and Caleb's body is strewn with chains like a mummy so as Belac can't hurt anyone. And so Cirena sends a small party of guards to retrieve Sceiro as fast as the wind allows, for she is in need of her requested forged relic.

Ichary teachs the werewolf clan and Oxgruf how ro forge weapons after she made werewolf smithing hammers. But then one night upon the full moon she falls ill and passes out and turns into a werewolf herself, though not quite as big as Oxgruf and the rest. When she reawakens as her normal self three days later she is furious when she learns of her transformation.

Ichary," you blockheads, where's Oxgruf i've got a bone to pick with his red furry ass!"

Clem," he's down by the river."

Ichary makes her way to the river where Oxgruf is fishing, he sees her coming his way … he pays no mind as he has no idea he should be alarmed. When she gets there she doesn't say a word, she lifts her sledgehammer way from way down low and blindsides Oxgruf with it.

Oxgruf," ah, what in the hell was that for?"

Ichary," what's it for what's it for you say … how bout the fact that i'm now a flea bitten mongrel you son of a bitch …"

Oxgruf," no you're not you're still the same Ichary."

Ichary," yea cept when its a full moon you bastard."

Oxgruf," are you serious, ich … I swear I had nothing to do with this, besides you've no bite or claw marks how can you be turned? There not even a neddle point mark so it wasn't done by blood."

Ichary," well then its the food, or clothing, or just being around you pricks, you're more contagious than you led me on to believe."

Oxgruf," and how's that a fault of mine, remember I've only been this way for a few years … how am I supposed to know you can't eat our food?"

Ichary," I don't know, but you better find a way to fix this god damn it."

Oxgruf," well the only way we're gonna get information about werewolves is relics records which is the assassins or the city state of light's records liabraries. And both places are not well off places to be.

Ichary," well get all your warriors ready cuz we're going to one of them and no it's not up to discussion."

Oxgruf," well far be it from me to question a woman scorned."

Cisaro, Salvic, and Torrin finally return to the dark and light citystate with their company bringing with them discreetly 3000 pounds of werewolf meat and Torrin picks the 30 least decayed ghuols to turn and support their cause. Meanwhile unbenonced of the unfolding events, Tarn torments Stayne in the lobby outside the throne room, while Mairlexa is away recruiting hunterclass fighters for the lord Lawrnev.

Tarn," look at those nasty whip lash cuts on your face, not so pretty anymore eh Stayne?"

Stayne," when I heal completely you'll be sorry Tarn, you boot licking creep … the only reason you out rank me is because of extenuating circumstances. Soon enough I'll outrank you again and then you'll be kissing my ass like before."

Tarn," yea but that won't be for a good long while, so for now shut it and be a good dog and fetch Lawrnev's dinner. And remember do it with a smile, lol."

Then Salvic and Torrin bring their group inside, to Tarn and Stayne's surprise. While Cisaro lingers in the crowd of vampire rebellion.

Tarn," what's this, who do you think you are coming in here like this, lord Lawrnev will not have such anarchy."

Torrin," this is a cudetah, choose a side now, ours … or death."

Stayne," I'll join."

Tarn," death who do you think you are lord lawrnev himself, get real ... I'm reporting this."

Salvic," you, you said you'll join ... disbatch of that one."

Tarn," what?"

Stayne," gladly."

Stayne though wounded, forces a sword through Tarns chest and then takes off his head with his bare hands. The group moves into the throneroom.

Lawrnev," well what's all this commotion I'm trying to get some rest."

Salvic," this is the end of your reign lord Lawrnev."

Lawrnev," oh is it now, and who do you suppose will lead this rabble roused motley crew of an empire, lol, you ... hahaha."

Cisaro steps to the front through the crowd," either pledge loyalty to me and step down, or die by my hand, I who was once Riscao."

Lawrnev," I think not, either fork over the relic dymo and I'll let you live or die and I'll take it off your corpse ... new management works just fine without you,"

Cisaro," what if I told you I could put you at the front of an army armed with endless relics, make you a real vampire lord with your own relic dymo and you can rule far more than just a city state? No one to answer to lest for me.

Lawrnev," promises from you are hollow."

Cisaro uses both the relic sphere and relic pyramid destroying both walls to the left and right.

Cisaro," bloodletter won't save you from my power, besides the relic dymo must be used properly which you have no idea how to do. Not only that, should you by chance win, the relic vampire will end you soon enough."

Lawrnev," relic vampire?"

Cisaro," yes, a being who devours relic weapons … and it is to my understanding he dies less easy than us … the choice is yours."

Squalaira," why don't you both share rule … two leaders if far better than one, think about it, an ancient master and a blood knowledged master working together as equals would make the realms easier to monopolize."

With no way to argue with her logic, both concede to a truce.

As Nexaug continues to battle for his life, a group of elder assassins grab him and inject him with multiple vials of their blood thats mixed with various poisons just like the half vampires inject him repeatedly with their infected vampire blood. After weeks upon weeks of this not knowing how much time has actually passed anymore Nexaug finds a secluded corner where he can rest, though he's out of toxic remedies and is overloaded with poisoned blood and vampire blood. It's at this time he begins to halucinate as the world spins around him, he can't seem to find an anchor to hold his racing thoughts down, he's become useless. Dresdin's turn to check on him as the betting pool continues, the pool has become so advanced even Nexaug's death is played.

Dresdin," yea he's down again, not sure if he's dead, if he is Barqua wins the lottery."

Dresdin checks Nexaugs pulse as Tristena watchs.

Tristena," well?"

Dresdin," still alive, counts as a spill down."

Tristena," fuck yea, I win the round, ear that shit Dresd … what the hell!"

Nexaug comes to his feet and grabs Dresdin and bites down on his jugular hard, sapping the blood from his body, Dresdin paralyzed can't move an inch or even speak. Tristena runs to report this to Barqua. By the time they return with a small contingent all that is left is Dresdin's lifeless body. The ruling class elite assassins were watching and waiting for just such an event and detained Nexaug in heavy chains.

Barqua," me thinks the game is over, shit just got real."

Tristena," I'm telling you he turned but in a bad way, I saw everything."

Barqua," I believe you."

In the secret catacombs of the basement of the assassins citadel the elder assassins prepere Nexaug's blood for experimentation. Navwec is also chained and bound to a chair as their patient one with Nexaug as patient zero. There are other assassins there chained as experimental effects of Nexaug's mutant vampire blood. The elder assassins are very meticulous and never leave anything to chance,

Feng," Nexaug's blood, patient zero, is being administered to Navwec and three other patients each with their own unique variables for posterity."

Mainge," patient zero seems to be highly aggitated constant, the need or maybe desire for blood has taken over his mind sadly to say."

Zarlo," the root of the need or desire needs to be understood so preparations and benefits to risk analysis can be discovered."

Renge," as well as the capabilities of this new strain of illness to ascertain it's cost and marketing as well as usability."

After Sceiro's private forging are complete, he makes known that Cirena wants relic weapons made by partners, two to a weapon forged extra.

Raize," why the extra work we have an arsenal at our disposal?"

Vailez," I agree what's the point to have such specific extra blades?"

Sceiro," It's called bllod brothers blades, the book says that in times of need the blade will come to the one who has need of it most during dire cicumstances, its like backup without the backup."

Korint," so what the weapons will have a conscience."

Zaila," does that mean the weapons will strike on their own?"

Sceiro," I'm not sure, she said the book wasn't too descriptive, but she said its worth having and not needing than needing and not having."

And so the blood brothers blades were made, even the halfblood vampires made some to test the theories. Korint and Zaila make one, Raize and Vailez make one and Sceiro makes one with Cirena's blood. When their work is completed, the whole army makes their return to the village as the guards reach them shortly after their return start. With the knowledge of Cirena's danger Sceiro returns through a portal.

As Mairlexa returns with her chosen vampire hunter class ghouls to have them turned she stumbles upon the diamond Fluoretta once possessed, which is the lunar diamond just as a pack of pure blood werewolves were to ambush her and her team. She fuses it into her chest as Fluoretta had and the ambushing werewolves become docile, the diamond allows her to command them. Forgetting her previous endeavors she brings them to Lawrnev's throne room.

Lawrnev," whats all this?"

Mairlexa," a diamond to control werewolves … better than hunterclass right."

Sceiro returns to the village with Cirena's requested watch relic as well as his and Cirena's bllod brothers blade, which Sceiro chose a shield blade.

Cirena," Caleb has returned but he's all wrong."

Sceiro," what do you mean?"

She shows him Caleb wrapped in chains.

Belac," when I free myself all those relics will be tasty."

Sceiro," you're not my brother."

Belac rips and breaks his bonds and attacks Cirena who is off guard. The blood brothers shield blade defends her. But but Belac manages to steal the time relic Sceiro brought her.

Belac," mmm … a fresh relic."

Cirena," no!"

Belac consumes it and two interdimensional tears open up one taking Belac and the other taking Sceiro.

Nexaug's halucinations turn into flashbacks of his memories. He is a late husband and father to two children.

Nexaug," Fluoretta come rend to Sceiro your little brother."

Fluoretta," coming, I have to go little one duty calls … be good for your parents Caleb."

Nexaug is speaking with an assassin.

Feng," Now is the time to fulfill your dury to the assassins code."

Nexaug tells Fluoretta to stay with her brother and be raised by Caleb's parents. But Fluoretta doesn't listen and goes her own path.

Nexaug flashs back to reality new poison and toxic serums were being fed to him.

Meinge," the four candidates plus a late addition all seem to have taken to the infection incredibly … healing rate increase and voratious feeders even compared to the halfblood vampires."

Renge," I've seen enough," takes four doses of Nexaugs blood himself.

Zarlo," I suppose you'll stand as the poison blooded immune test."

Feng," if your transformation is anything like the candidates we will join you,"

Ichary sees the next full moon and changes into a werewolf but not senseless and wild this time. Her relic is disintegrating and as her body absorbs it it is curing her of the mindlessness of her change and it allows her to change at will.

Ichary," well now talk about some luck, this is a little more acceptable."

Oxgruf," thats a bit of luck I do say so, maybe you won't kill me now."

Ichary," I think not."

Meanwhile the ground where Fluoretta died grows a massive lotus flower. Purple is its color. And five years past since her death the lotus opens in bloom with a naked Fluoretta emerging.

Fluoretta," never would've thought that a relic users dearh would have a rebirth so unique."

The power of herbomancy at her disposal she moves tp Ironside village to find Sceiro to have another relic weapon made for her.

Warping through vortexs pulls the fractured being Caleb into three separate people. First Belac rips out of Caleb's body, then Labec comes out. The process is all very violent and causes all three enormous amounts of pain. They come to the end of the vortex, Caleb is thrown off mid vortex to god who knows where. Labec and Belac both fell out at the end onto an alien planet in a strange solar system. The missing Caleb who becomes Riscao was transported to the past where he controlled the city of darkness and light.

Belac," i am no friend to you."

Labec," well if you're looking for a fight now, I can accomadate you."

Belac uses a pryamid relic to fire bullets at Labec, who earthmances trees as a shield. Belac runs off to hide. Leaving Labec to explore the planet. There are strange yellow trees, purple water, and red rocks. Then he comes under attack by a pride of tigers. The only relic he has left is the four pointed star relic he found on the island with the spirit. He uses it, its a cosmic relic … moving meteors to crash into the tigers.

Andrew (time indian, king of indian law)," hey who are you, oh hey you're you who else would you be, haha."

Sceiro," where am I, who are you."

Andrew," who me, oh I'm Andrew the Time indian, we are in another dimension outside of time. I'm an ancient guardian of the fabric of reality or something like that."

Sceiro," Wait my relics where are they?"

Andrew," oh you mean these things … yea sorry in the void outside of time things like this aren't allowed."

Electricity sparks from Andrew's fingertips and lightening strikes everywhere around them.

Sceiro," I don't understand how do I get out of here … to get back to where I was?"

Andrew," well you can't use these cause like you know I just said these here are a serious no no … their use could trigger the unmaking of all realities."

Sceiro," but I need their power to be able to do what I do, without them Im nothing."

Andrew," listen, these things don't have power, only the power you give em. And if you want outta here you'll have to do it like an indian."

Sceiro," what do you mean like an indian."

Andrew summons forth power and creates a massive solar system and torques its reality. Spinning the star around and inbetween planets. Then he forces reality to put them inside it in the middle of the desert.

Andrew," here you will learn how to control infinites without the use of relic devices."

Andrew makes a firepit then builds a teepe around it.

Andrew," this is the hotbox, inside you will have fire and water. You must use them both correctly to do this. This will bring your body temperature way up and send you into visions. It is there you must take control of matter and bend it to your will, just don't bend too hard."

Ichary," we're going down there I don't care how many ghouls there are, I want answers."

Ichary and the werewolf tribe go to the city state of dark and light and raid the section where the liabrary of knowledge and records sits. The ghouls are easy trgets to overpower especially with the werewolves in their new armor outfitted with weapons. Though to no avail, werewolves are fairly new to the realm, there is no information about their transformations there is no information on werewolves at all. So Ichary has another idea.

Ichary," then its to the assassin's citadel to look at their records there has to be something on all this somewhere."

Oxgruf," if there's nothing here, what makes you think there'll be anything at the assassin's citadel?"

Ichary," cause if there's nothing to educate me, you'll face my whip again deary."

Oxgruf," oh no."

Meinge," Nexaug's test subjects have such improved abilities in different ways. One very fast and heals quickly, one one big strong and capable of breaking swords, another that is highly intelligent, and one other that sees in the dark."

Zarlo," and Feng's age appears to be reversing, not only is immortallity here but the fountain of youth so to speak."

Nexaug," what you're doing is bad, you don't know what will come of this."

Feng," I do, the new future … lol."

Renge," half of the guard should remain human … turn only the older and wiser of our people."

Ichary's raid left big losses for the city state of dark and light, as well as an infurious Lawrnev.

Lawrnev," look at what this partnership has brought … open war in which we're losing."

Cisaro," I have nothing to do with the werewolves attack. Maybe if you hadn't hunted them to the brink."

Lawrnev," enough," stabs cisaro through the heart with bloodletter, but can't pull it out.

As Lawrnev tries to pull out bloodletter Cisaro's body consumes the blade til there is nothing but the hilt left.

Lawrnev," how can this happen?"

Cisaro," because I am a relic vampire, I can not be killed by a relic weapon … at least not an ordinary one."

Lawrnev," so then you die harder than my kind."

Cisaro," yes, and with every relic I consume so does my Knowledge broaden. The blood in the relics can be very old and gives me insight to things of the past."

Lawrnev," that was my vampire blade it fed me knowledge like that, and now its gone."

Cisaro," then you shouldn't have stabbed me with it."

Lawrnev," I wanted to taste your blood's knowledge."

Cisaro," It matters not, we can build new ones now … consuming a relic also enables me to know how to forge it."

Lawrnev," really, an army of bloodletter blade weilding vampires."

And so hundreds of bloodletter swords were forged in the vampire citadel. Making an army so formitable all fear the idea of war.

Meanwhile Labec tracks down Belac and enters a temple maze to fight with Belac. But Labec gets lost in the maze after one fight the two had. And as Labec makes his way through the maze, Belac comes to a room where he meets Joe the indian of correct placement, who knows the exact right place everything and everyone are supposed to be.

Joe," um, hello."

Belac," who are you and what do you do."

Joe," I'm Joe, I do this."

Joe sends him through a portal and he and Cisaro switch places and Cisaro was sent to the temple maze, where he meets with Labec who he trades blows with and and Labec kills him in an epic fight where neither of their relic weapons worked so it was a hand to hand fight with whatever weapons they could find off hand. Cisaro found an ax and Labec picked up a broad sword in mid fray. Cisaro fought hard but took a stab to the heart just before Labec beheaded him. Then Labec makes his way through the maze trying to find the way to return to his world. He stumbles across Joe the indian.

Joe," hey you where do you want to go?"

Labec," what?"

Joe," you're already in both places of where you should be. I wasn't sure of what to do so I fugured I'd send you where ever you wanted to go. So where you headed."

Labec," back to Cirena's camp."

Andrew monitors Sceiro's progress in the hot box, Sceiro sweats profusely.

Sceiro," dude its like a million degrees in here and i got no vision whats the deal."

Andrew," drip water on the coals to make steam, it needs to be hotter but a wet hot."

So Sceiro abides Andrew's instructions while sipping some of the water for himself. Eventually Sceiro begins to halucinate from the heat. Flashs of memories hit Sceiro, at this point Andrew enters the hot box.

Andrew," don't focus on your memories that'll hold you back everytime. Instead embrace the chaos for what it is chaotic order. Then focus on designing cosmic bodies … like this …"

Andrew torques reality and creates an entire mini solar system.

Sceiro," wha.,,t.?"

Andrew," this is cosmic build, creation law."

Sceiro," to do what."

Andrew," this," flings the cosmic solar system, he feeds upon the energy from it and puts his fist through the ground.

Sceiro," so you create things like that to provide yourself with power."

Andrew," exactly, but you can also gain knowledge from this practice as well, there's alot of math involved give it a shot."

Sp Sceiro does and creates a planet that geo hammers itself to become more massive, a highly dangerous starting point.

Sceiro," hiyagh."

All reality begins to warp and grind upon itself.

Andrew," woah, back it off dude it only takes a little thought!"

Sceiro," i can't."

So Andrew starts creating counter gravity pulling star systems one after another til gravity equalizes.

Andrew," man I thought you might understand but you need these relics, they're like bonds to channel your power through, so you should stay here to learn how to do things without such crutchs."

Sceiro," I think I have it down well enough, while reality was getting chewed up my eye of convolution gave me the understanding of how it works."

Andrew," thats because its not a relic, its an indian law rech device."

Sceiro," you could help me out better if you returned with me, my people are in the middle of war."

Andrew," I can't, I've had my time ... this is your time to live, helping you in that way is forbidden ... unless another like me is involved, my hands are tied. The thing is that you have to understand is that this power you have isn't anything unique or special. All who live are capable of willing law tech to their preference, you just have to understand how and why."

Sceiro," so vampires and werewolves aren't unnatural to my world for you to do anything about."

Andrew," no, i only get involved if an indian law being infringes on the life tech's reality and endangers it. Like what this watch represents. It'll allow you move through time and more, which is very dangerous to life tech and the flow of reality itself."

Sceiro," are you saying I won't get it back."

Andrew," you can have it back when you understand how to use it properly. I suggest crushing it to powder and consumption of its knowledge."

Sceiro," what will that do?"

Andrew," give you a natural ability to torque time itself … or kill you, not ezactly too sure … lol."

Cirena thumbs through her spell book to find a way to keep Caleb and his monsters from consuming relics the way they do. She finds the entrapment of darkness spell. So she paints the ground with an ancient alchemy spell circle and chants the magic words.

Cirena," that which is evil and wrong be it so that it is traped in a song and be isolated away for a very long."

And so Belac is trapt within a new magic spell relic … one of the requested items on Cirena's list of relic work Sceiro had done.

Shortly after the assassins perfected the mutated vampire serum, they drive the half bloods out of the citadel. And with no where to go the half bloods join with the others with Raize's group. Around this time Nexaugs body goes into shock and he dies strapped to the table in the assassins medical room. He is placed in a concrete tonb to preserve his body, which is lucky for him who awakens from death as a new mutated vampire.

Fluoretta happened upon Cirena as she was searching for Sceiro to make a new relic weapon since her last one was taken.

Cirena," can I help you miss."

Fluoretta," Fluor, I'm no miss sweetie ... and help, yea maybe. Do you know anyone named Sceiro in this village?"

Cirena," Sceiro, he's my friend, but he's not here ... off dealing with things I know not of."

Fluoretta," damn, I need his skilled hands to make me a new relic."

Cirena," did you say relic ... i can help you there."

Fluoretta," how?"

Cirena," this book is about everything relic."

The two thumb through the tome as Cirena explains the process for making good relics.

Fluoretta," so its that simple huh."

Cirena," yes, you can make a good relic yourself, in fact selfmade relics are better."

Fluoretta," then I'm off to build a better relic."

Cirena," here take these copies of relic symbols with you, they'll provide your relic with extra power."

As Fluoretta leaves the village Raize and his company return with their hard earned work.

Back in the city state of light and dark Lawrnev scowls over the disappearance of Cisaro, who enabled his army to be equiped with bloodletter relic blades.

Lawrnev," where is that fool its as if I run the whole show myself like before … to hell with him we'll launch an attack at the assassins we need more territory."

And so Lawrnev's forces invaded the assassin's territory. It was a war Lawrnev's forces were pushed back but the vampires found that the new vampire mutants blood was like a drug that made them stronger. And so Lawrnev decided to put his bloodletter army together for raids and capture of mutated vampires.

Raize and his group upon returning to the village found Oxgruf's werewolf tribe attempting to make peace with them and the other surrounding villages. But Raize's group only saw a threat of a werewolf invasion and drove them out. So then Ichary visited the village since she retained her human form to discuss peace.

Vailez," so you're with the werewolves?"

Ichary," yes and they want you to understand that you have no need to be threatened by them, they just want to live normal lives like the rest of us."

Raize," well their appearance doesn't instill thoughts of warm kittens … but I can understand where they're coming from."

Ichary," they also would like to open up trade with you."

Raize," we'll start with peace and go from there."

Elsewhere Lawrnev's forces meet the vampire assassins in battle.

Mairlexa," nothing like an old dust up to get the blood flowing, with the werewolves at my disposal the assassins don't stand a chance."

But she was wrong, the new mutated vampires were too strong. And Lawrnev's forces were pushed back ... for every vampire assassin wounded spurned a new mutated vampire as their blood was highly infectious. Including Mairlexa who was turned when ambushed moving to the front line to command the werewolves. And so now the werewolves are fighting for the assassins.

Meanwhile Sceiro was busy training with Andrew.

Sceiro," this hot box thing, I'm getting used to it. I'm getting the hang of this cosmic build thing too."

Andrew," yea, just remember its about balancing the gravity so things don't get torqued beyond your intentions ... are you ready to consume this watch relic?"

Sceiro builds a massive solar system and fires it in one direction as Andrew places the watch in front of Sceiro. Sceiro absorbs the energy from the torquing cosmic and crushes the watch into powder. Then he snorts the watch dust and time knowledge floods his mind. He sees the past and all the events that lead up to his time. Wars, disease, and mutations. Then he starts to see the future, which is chaotic at first ... then he sees more clearly. His people in a war, his friends all enslaved and innocent people tortured on a routine basis. Then he sees how the past. Present, and future are all connected. Then he sees that there's nothing that can be done as time is just a force much like gravity, when tampered with it must be balanced with a counter weight.

Andrew," yeah but you'll never get back in time to stop what will happen ... it takes time to return from this place."

Sceiro," we'll see about that, my people will not live that way."

Sceiro builds massive galaxies to propel him through a portal to take him back. When he returns to where he left at Cirena's village, he sees nothing but devastation all around. Everyone was either killed or captured as slaves being tortured by Nexaug and his mutant vampire followers, sceiro finds Cirena locked in a cage forced to watch as her relic tome is force fed to Labec who is actually Caleb's still maimed mind. Which causes him to become a relic vampire with no hope of return for either of them as Cirena is bound to the book and page by page once completely consumed she will die. Sceiro tries to stop it, but Stayne gets in his way as Nexaug watches in delight. So Sceiro thinks time, I'll change what happened. And so he cosmic builds multiple galaxies and torque pushes his way to the past. Sceiro arrives back at Cirena's village the same time Raize and his company return.

Cirena," Sceiro!"

Caleb/Labec also arrived at the same time

Caleb/Labec," finally together again."

Sceiro," get ready for war lest we all die!"

Sceiro explains everything to them. And so Raize clls upon the werewolf tribe to join, which they do. And so they marched, first to the citadel of light and dark whose forces were beaten back and combined forces. Then to the assassins citadel where battle commenced. Sceiro's forces equiped with relic blades, fighting Mairlexa's enslaved werewolves were the blood brothers relic weapons as well as is they were in dire need of. And using the werewolf tribe as a shield because they were immune to Nexaug's mutant vampire force, the army of humans and half bloods take down all who oppose them as Sceiro, Caleb/Labec, Raize, and Vailez battle and maim Nexaug who unlike the rest can't be killed so they dismember and behead him and have each part locked in a tomb of its own. Sceiro going back in time caused a reality grind in the time he came from. So Andrew indian king shows up.

Andrew," you massively tore up reality with your time stunt. By rights I should undo your work but it turns out to be the right path to alter the events in time … at least this time."

About the Author

James G. Mahoney Jr. grew up in Gloucester City, New Jersey, until age eleven when his he moved with his father to the rural suburbs of Atco. After attending college for a short time, James worked in the construction trade for several years. He currently resides in Hammonton, New Jersey. Journey of the Red Blooded is his first book.